INTIMATE ENEMIES

ROBERT FURST & ALAN PARKER

ISBN: 978-0692694763

ISBN-0692694765

TABLE OF CONTENTS

ACKNOWLEDGMENTS

We want to thank our moms for their patience, our two cats –
Fluffy & Clark Kent for giving us a reason to keep writing
and keep them in cat food, our girlfriends who put up with
our late night brainstorming sessions and the universal muse
that keeps giving us ideas.

We would also like to thank Fiction Buzz Press for allowing
us to join the collective in order to get our fiction works out
there. What a great group of writers to work with.

PROLOGUE

The secret police are everywhere; they invade your dreams like ants at a picnic. You don't always see them, but you always see the results of their handiwork.

Run, Aleksandra, run away before the big, bad man comes and takes you away. I react immediately to the voice screaming at me. It's my mother, and she is being drug out of our warm home into the street by faceless men in black uniforms. I follow her instructions, narrowly missing one of these black monsters as they swoop down and try to grab me.

The dreamscape shifts and I am outside, watching my father, brothers and my mother lined up in front of the stone wall that surrounds our home. It is cold, blindingly white snow frozen by the arctic winter cold, and they're wearing only pants and shirts. No shoes, no coats. I shiver with them as the secret police pace up and down screaming at them.

"Where is your girl, Aleksandra," one of them screams. My mother is weeping softly, and my heart constricts in empathetic pain. My teeth chatter in the freezing chill and my ears hurt; my lips are blue tinged, and the cold seeps into the pockets where I have stuffed my hands against the numbing freeze. The screaming man holds a gun up to my mother's head. His intent is clear; either produce me or she will die. He starts counting backwards: I can hear him plain as day: десять, девять, восемь…10, 9, 8….

I can't let my family die.

"семь, шесть . . .7, 6… "

I start running across the field towards my family. I know my mother told me to run away, but if I run, she will die. I can't let her die. She's my mother. I can't let any of them die. They're my family. I see the bad men, the secret police my mother called them, turn watching me running through the field.

My mother starts screaming, and I realize she's screaming at me to run away. She sounds frantic, desperate and inconsolable, but for once, I cannot follow her orders. I can't let them kill my family; no matter what happens to me.

The man in charge laughs, and slaps my mother across the face. I continue coming closer, she keeps screaming and then I hear the shots. They crack into the air like thunder without the storm. My family falls like marionettes whose strings have been cut – slowly, dramatically, one at a time. The shots come again. The noise reverberates in my ears, ringing out across the hills.

My father falls ever so slowly, sinking to his knees, his eyes ablaze looking directly at me, then they soften and like a candle, life is extinguished in them. He sinks the rest of the way to the ground, falling sideways like a sack of potatoes. Except he isn't a sack of produce. He is, he was my father who loved me and told me stories about happier times in our little village. Now, he is dead, and I scream my agony at them as I close the distance between us.

Again the shots ring out, and my mother falls, then finally, my big brothers, who are so strong, and who have teased me and protected me my whole life, jerk from the impact of the bullets and fall forward, still.

I watch with shocked horror at the blood turning the beautiful white snow dark red, a stark contrast between white and red, against life and death.

I scream. I screech. I wail as I come upon them. I want to kill them, but I am just a girl and they are big, strong men. They slap me, push me and finally carry me fighting blindly to a waiting car, shoving me in the back with laughs and jibes about my now dead family. I rage and scream, and finally, after what seems like a very long time, I sink into silence.

The corpse of my beloved mother is talking to me. "We were dead the day you left, my beloved Aleksandra. Do not believe what they tell you. We were a liability, something for you to hold on to. They killed us as soon as your car disappeared over the horizon. If you have found love, true love, then run, Aleksandra, run like you never have before. Because, you are just as expendable as we are, and when they have what they want, they will kill you, too."

I hear the voice of my father echoing my mother's warning, "Run, Aleksandra, run for your life, and don't look back."

"This is what happens when you fail in your mission, comrade," the captain and leader of these monsters is screaming at me, but I know he is lying. "You have fallen in love with an American, and in doing so, you have failed your country, embarrassed your trainers and killed your family."

As we drive across the countryside, I vow to wreak vengeance on these men. They will pay for what they've done to my family. They will all pay one day when they least expect it. They will underestimate me, because I am a girl. And, that will be there undoing.

I have always had visions about the future, and they have

always come true. I imagine my captors deaths in a myriad of ways as we drive towards our destination – all of them horrific, all of them vile – just like the men who perpetuated my family's demise.

All I am is hatred; all I am is rage, and while they plot to get me to do their bidding, I plot to be the instrument of their end. The visions give me cold comfort and fortify me against the pain that sweeps across my soul in waves. I know that when the time is right, I will run, but first I will kill all of those who have destroyed my world.

***

I wake up in my bed shivering, shaking and frantic. *Where am I? What happened?* The pain in my chest is gripping; I'm choking with the grief of it. It's dark, cold and I am alone.

Only I'm not alone.

I am in the bed of one of the most powerful men in American politics, poised to run for president in the coming years. And, he loves me with all of my faults and insecurities.

He wraps his arms around me asking me about my night terrors. I don't respond. How can I? I am supposed to betray this man, to pass all of his secrets along to my homeland, Mother Russia. It is why they trained me, why they sent me to the United States and into his arms.

There's only one problem with their plan; they were right in my vision, but they will find out too late. I am head over heels in love with an American, and the thought of betraying him is no longer in my playbook. I will do anything to protect him, even risk certain death and betrayal of my own country. I know the secret they hold over me – I know my family is already dead. There is nothing they can do to me that's worse than my vision.

He kisses me on the back of my neck, whispering soft reassurances. "I love you, Alex," he whispers in my ear. "You can tell me anything, you know that don't you?"

"Yes," I whisper softly, but I know it's a lie. If I tell him who I really am and what I'm supposed to be doing, he will leave me faster than I can say 'hot diggity dog.' That's his expression, not mine. "I love you, too."

CHAPTER ONE

"The tragedy of this world is that no one is happy, whether
stuck in a time of pain or of joy." – Alan Lightman

March 1961

The winds off the Irtysh are cold and wet, turning the river
water into snowflakes that feel like they're cutting into my
reddened cheeks. The fields and the sky are white and endless;
only a thin, distant horizon to separate them. My blonde hair
fades into the pale surroundings, and even though I've finally
grown up enough to be seen as a young woman and no longer
a child to everyone except those in my own family, I still feel
small against the expanse of the Omskaya oblast.

Papa is waiting for me back at the house, far from the
romance and culture of Omsk city, where the Trans-Siberian
Railway, the airport and the river port brought all of Siberia
together in a frenzy of trade, goods and gossip. It would have

been the Siberian capital if it weren't for Novosibirsk, but Omsk still thrives, the air cradling grey clouds from the natural gas and oil mines.

And a lot of that oil is buried deep in Papa's face; his fingers, the crags of his wrists and elbows and neck; thin black veins that seem to run just above the skin. I know he never smiles when he's working the oil mines. In fact, he only ever really smiles at me. His lips break wide across his tired face, the wrinkles gathering at the corners of his eyes as he stretches his arms out to me. "Sandra," he always calls me. Aleksandra can be turned into so many nicknames, but they all sound basically the same to me; I'll always be Aleksandra Zolotov, no matter what they call me.

But Papa never smiles at Gregory or Vlad. I know he loves them, of course; they're his sons and his eldest children. Perhaps it is because he wants to make sure they grow up strong and solid and proud that he treats them so coldly. But that is not what Papa wants for me.

And what I want for myself is a new question that follows me on my long walks through the snowfields. I think about my childhood here, filled with so many hours of dancing and singing and make-believe in these very fields, when my head is filled with visions of princes and adventure.

I thrill to the possibilities of my unknown future. I know that danger will await me no matter where I go; somehow I even want it to. I yearn for the excitement of the outside world, of the pain and pleasure and all that being alive can mean. I am young and desirable, and I will have enemies that will pursue me in any event. But my family will be safe. And whatever danger awaits me, I only hope that I won't be facing it alone.

And that is all I ever really want.

Mamma always tries to warn me about being lost in such dreams, that I have a duty to find a husband and serve him, give him children and to accept that he is not be a prince, but a hard-working and respectable man. Anything else is foolishness, and she warns me that it could bring me to ruin.

But there is always Papa, protecting his daughter against any opposition, even under our own roof. "Why must you taunt the child?" he's say to Mamma, more a command than a question. To his sons, he'd say worse.

And I walk through the whip of the cold, vast fields off the river; I look around and know that Mamma had been right. I am still grateful for my Papa's dedication to me, of course. No matter where I go or what happens to me, I will always be his daughter. But there isn't any future for me here but a life of service to a man whose own life is spent in the service of some other man, whose life is similarly wasted in service to someone else. Somebody somewhere did not serve another; but that man served the Siberian people. And I'd never meet such a man in the dreary chill of the Omsk.

My mind flashes on a series of images; people I have never met, places I have never been. An ugly man with a pronounced ridge over his eyes, brows thick and tangled, snarling at my mind's eye; then he grins. Another flash, this one of a young woman, naked and twisting from the end of a chain.

No, not a young woman.

A young man.

Another image bursts in my brain, shivers running down my spine and not from the cold, snowy wind. I see a city, speckled with light against an inky night's sky.

Moscow? No. Somewhere in America? New York?

I can't be certain. I have never seen Moscow or New York. I can only dream and conjure what they might look like. We are poor; there are no books. All that I have learned is from my mamma, who has dutifully taught me my letters, words, arithmetic and the domestic arts: cooking, cleaning, knitting and quilting against the cold. Our existence is more pleasant than some of our neighbors. My father and brothers work hard to ensure that my belly is full, our house warm and life congenial. It is safe, secure and to me, utterly boring.

I have always had a gift; my mother has told me. I have seen images, visions that are many times proven real. These aren't the first images of their kind to find a home in my heated imagination. Ever since I was a little girl, I've been receptive to these images, pictures of moments in time that hadn't yet happened, but were going to; or were happening even then, miles away. Even when I was an infant, they say I cried terribly whenever something bad happened in the neighborhood even before we'd heard about it. They say I was in hysterics the day the Hawaiian port of Pearl Harbor was bombed, even though I was only one year old and we had no news of the event until sometime later.

When I was a little girl, I had visions of that terrible wall the Germans just built this year in the center of their capital city, Berlin. It looked exactly in my mind as it does now; sections of concrete and barbed wire, towers and guards and dogs and searchlights.

Nobody could ever explain my visions, and often I can't even understand them until later, when their meaning sometimes becomes clear. They hit me as abstract images, flashes of nervous energy that spill out in front of my mind's eye with terrible quickness, like steel blades cutting through my brain and my heart.

But there is no questioning the realness of my prophecies or their accuracy. Even now I'm haunted by suggestions of things to come which I know I cannot stop even when I am given warning of their terrible approach; like a train cutting through the flat flesh of the Siberian landscape, steadily getting louder and closer.

I see the flash of another face, once again one I don't recognize. This is often the case with my visions, but not always. I don't care to remunerate on it because the visions have never brought me anything other than pain and dread. I have never mastered the visions; they have always been my master. So this face, like so many others, comes and goes in an inexplicable moment, a heartbeat of the mind. It is a strong face, angular, drawn and pale. Sad. Scared.

I approach the house, one of several on a quiet road stretching through the endless white. Gregory and Vlad shovel snow from the street. Their tall, broad frames stand out against the white powder around them, heavy wool coats wrapped around them. They glare at me as I approach, then look at each other and shake their heads.

"The snow princess returns," Gregory says, his blue eyes flashing.

Vlad looks at me and adds, "Did you capture the wolf today, young Peter?"

"Perhaps if you picked up a shovel once or twice yourself," Gregory says to me, "you'd prove yourself worthy of a husband!"

They laugh, but I am not amused.

I have already had plenty of attention from young men, and some that were not young at all. Shopkeepers, teachers, classmates; all have shown interest in my time, my body. I know my limbs are strong but still lithe, graceful. I know my face has a certain softness that boys have always liked to look at, to touch, to kiss.

But not everybody wanted merely to kiss. And I have wanted more than that myself on many occasions.

It is not always so cold in the Omsk.

Not that I want to share my experiences in the barns and the fields and the shadows while dancers twirled and men drank. These are my private experiences, winsome highlights of a childhood a lot people would mourn, even if my own brothers envy it. But the life of every young woman includes time with young men; their hands clumsy, fingers groping, tongues that lack subtlety, much less mastery.

Or restraint.

There had been that one night, after the celebration of the

birthday of Peter the Great, when two of the gas minors found me out in the field, alone, further out than any scream could carry.

But Gregory had arrived before clothes had been stripped away, before my neck had been cut or my belly slit open. And his attack upon them had been vicious, anger roaring out of his mouth as he picked up one and threw him into the other like some mad giant.

After that, my brothers started watching me more and more and the boys came around less and less. Soon, only trusted elders were allowed within reach of me before one or more of my guardians would interfere. As I neared my twenties, and then stepped daintily into them, an aura of inapproachability had cut me off from the men of our neighborhood, and a lot of that had to do with my brothers' overprotectiveness.

So, to tease me about it is not only hurtful, but misguided. I look at Vlad, my lips small between my cheeks, chin jutted slightly as I look him over. "I had a vision of you, Vlad, last night."

Vlad's smile melts away as silence replaces their callous chortles. "What?" Vlad asks. "Tell me, what was it, what did you see?"

I hadn't seen anything the night before, no visions of Vlad

or anyone else. But that doesn't mean I'm above letting him squirm on the hook of my birthright. I just look him over, my expression solemn, my eyes combing his supposedly doomed frame. Without a word, I turn and walk into the house.

Vlad bolts after me, Gregory pushing against his chest to stop him from falling upon me from behind. "Tell me what you saw, you witch!"

"Vladimir," Gregory says, "don't you know when she's pulling your leg?"

"That's easy for you to say, Gregory. It wasn't you she had the vision of." By then I am in the house, but I can still hear Gregory's voice, muffled from outside. "Am I to die, Aleksandra?"

In the house, Mamma hovers over the stove, beet soup boiling in a cast-iron pot. She looks at me, her posture stooped from years tending to that pot and that stove, those beets and soups lovingly prepared for her husband and children.

Is this what I want for myself? I have to wonder, and not for the first time.

Her face is craggy with worry, hair lifeless and limp as it falls down over her forlorn brow. She looks at me and gives me a wordless kiss on the cheek. She turns away, with even more melancholy than usual, the silent tension even heavier around her than it has always been.

"Mamma?" I ask, not needing to say more.

"Aleksandra," Papa says from the other room as he enters. He is not smiling, but his arms are outstretched.

I fall into his loving grip and let him squeeze me, as always. And yet, it is not as it has always been. Something feels off, it feels somehow wrong. His embrace feels less like it is welcoming me in than bidding me farewell. He squeezes extra tight, as if somehow he knows I am slipping through his fingers.

I'd noticed changes in him over the years, of course, for every father must change as their little children become adults and prepare for lives of their own. Gregory and Vlad were both working the oil mines with Papa, and at twenty-one I am still at a marriageable age.

We aren't children anymore.

But we are still a family, and always would be, no matter where our travails take us. Like a lot of families, the future lay in togetherness. The further we travelled, the less likely we would ever be to return or to see the others again. Siberia is a big place, Russia even bigger and the whole world bigger still.

It is easy to get lost in such a place.

So families like ours tend to stay together, huddled up against the snow and the cold and the bleak world of danger and solitude, loneliness and despair; a desolate landscape that consumes the hapless and wayward.

I ease back out of Papa's arms. He lets go slowly, reluctantly, as if he knows he'll never be able to hold me again. "Papa?" I ask, turning back toward my mother to repeat the question that lingered unanswered from moments before. "Mamma, what is it? What's happened?"

Papa walks over to the little kitchen table and raises a thin, folded newspaper, our local gazette. Even from across the room, I recognize the initials in the subhead above the article.

KGB.

For people like us, that usually means one thing.

Death.

A wave of nervous terror ripples through my body, shaking me to my core. Even in the warmth of the kitchen, I feel chilled to the bone, despite the air filled with steam from the boiling soup, the acrid smell of cabbage in my skull.

I notice Gregory and Vlad enter from outside. Vlad's anger

has melted away.

He's already heard the bad news, whatever it is.

They all have.

I let my eye fall to the newspaper, knowing the printed words wouldn't share my family's reticence. As the black print seems to hover above the trembling gray sheet in my hand, my brain struggled to wrap itself around their terrible meaning.

Words like official invitation, compulsory, subject to arrest.

Daughter or daughters.

I can scarcely keep my brain going in a single direction, much less control it enough to digest the hideous truth behind the words.

"Papa?"

"It's another one of their schemes! The KGB won't make a whore of my daughter!"

"Not a whore, Papa," Gregory says. "A spy."

Vlad looks at me, almost smiling. "Perhaps, your visions will do you some good after all."

Mamma rushes over to me, wrapping her arms around my

head. "Tell them nothing of it, Aleksandra, promise me! Promise you'll tell them nothing! Be a good girl, do as you're told and tell them nothing."

"She'll not do as she's told," Papa says, "because she'll not be there."

"We haven't got any choice, Papa," Vlad says. "It's the gulag for us all if she doesn't go."

"You coward," Papa yells at him. "You've always despised her!"

"We are the ones who have been protecting her, looking out for your precious wood nymph as she prances around with the spirits. All the while she's danced herself over a cliff and you haven't the eyes to see it. Who is the coward now, Papa?"

Papa lunges at Vlad, the two men clashing in the center of the room. Papa's fingers crane around Vlad's neck, their faces red, veins pushing up along their necks as their strength is suddenly pitted against one another.

Mamma pulls at Papa, her tiny hands gripping his wool sweater. Gregory pushes himself between the two men, hands on each of their chests as he struggles to push them apart.

Our family, which has always been so tightly knit and self-reliant, is suddenly tearing itself apart.

And I am the reason for it, even if I am not necessarily to blame.

And only I can stop this conflict.

"Stop," I shout, "both of you please, stop this fighting! Papa!" My voice finally cuts through the waves of tension breaking between the jagged rocks that are my father and brother. They all look at me, standing by the kitchen table just outside the scramble of their fracas.

Calm returns to the kitchen, their eyes upon me. Gregory manages to push the other two away from each other, Mamma's hands still clinging to Papa's back.

I say, "It's okay, I'll go."

"No!" Papa shouted. "You have no idea what you're talking about! You'll be disappeared, Sandra, given over to men who -- "

"I'm not a child anymore, Papa. I know what men are, and what they're capable of."

Vlad says, "Child, you have no idea what a man is capable of."

But I do know. My brothers have been protective, and they'd been attentive. But they haven't been entirely effective.

I know.

I had visions, this time of myself; quick flashes of my face, twisted in agony, smeared with grime, sweating, sobbing.

Dying.

I say, "I'm sure it will be fine, everyone. What an opportunity to help Mother Russia." I have never used that expression before, and I hope it doesn't reveal to them that I am lying, and very poorly too.

"What good thing has the KGB ever done?" Papa asks anyone with the courage to answer. "There's no light at the end of this tunnel, and you've have me hurl the jewel of this family into that abyss?"

I can see that my father's anger will soon get the better of him, and he'll find himself at the hurtful end of a private KGB meeting of his own.

I try to smile when I say, "You all know there's no future for me here, no husband or adventure. Perhaps this wolf is really a sheep."

"Adventure!" Mamma says, a lifetime of it finally toppling down and crushing her. "I told you what madness you were bringing down upon yourself with your whimsies and your foolishness."

"Without them," I snap back, "why bother to live at all?"

"Young Peter," Vlad says to Gregory, both shaking their heads.

Gregory turns to me with a smile. "We shall go together, as a family. This wolf will get as much as he can handle."

I try to smile back, my genuine gratitude for his support and love not quite counteracting my own creeping sense of misery and dread. It's true, I don't see much life for myself in the Omsk, but in the KGB all I can really see for myself is death.

Torture, then death.

I say to Papa, "You can't stop me!" Being my father's only daughter has some perks, among them his strong, almost instinctual compulsion to give in to my will. And although I don't think of myself as spoiled and certainly not as privileged, I do realize that I've learned from more than one experiment that my father is most likely to stand behind me, beside me, in front of me; anywhere but against me. To him alone, I say, "Please don't make me stay in the Omsk, to grow old and tired. Don't keep me cooped up here anymore."

Silence fills the room in the absence of any answer. I can feel my Papa's heart breaking to have me deny his love and protectiveness and refuse his dedication. I love my home and I don't feel cooped up in it at all. But the sorrow of feeling that he'd brought me pain is a much lesser evil than the pain he'd feel knowing how terrified and sad I am to be saying goodbye to my family, almost certainly for ever more.

CHAPTER TWO

"The mystery of human existence lies not in just staying alive, but in finding something to live for." -- Fyodor Dostoyevsky

April 1961

We all travel together to the city of Omsk. Local magistrates send buses to the surrounding towns to make sure that the smaller, outlaying populations complies with the government's official invitation. The threat of death was not enough. A show of guns in the hands of young guardsmen, sent as escorts, and flat gray buses that arrived empty and left full more than did the trick.

The drive takes hours and the road is rocky, the bus weaving and swaying around us. There are three buses ahead of us and four behind, but none can be seen nor heard for the whipping winds and the thickening snow flurries. Inside the bus, there is an ominous murmur that borders on silence. The armed guard in the back of the bus glares at those who dare to mutter to one another, even to mother's when their sorrow overtakes their composure.

Papa glares at them, Mamma solemnly at me. Gregory and Vlad remain at home, unable to secure passage onboard the overcrowded bus.

When we arrive, the streets are already overflowing with our neighbors, some we know and some we do not. Families huddle around their young daughters, some as young as fourteen or even younger. Mothers sob, men stand stoically nodding to each other, each hopping that neither daughter is taken from them and both hoping that, if it must happen, that it happen to the other.

We get out of the bus; the smell of fear is potent. It smells like copper, like old vegetables, and it rots the wind cutting through the streets of downtown Omsk, our so-called *Siberian Chicago.*

Omsk is already home to over a million Siberians, many well-educated and productively employed. The influx of what looks like thousands of us from the surrounding areas, the oil and gas mining families, the farmers and ranchers, gives the romance of the big city an over-crowded, impoverished aspect.

The smell of the passing automobiles is strong in the air,

even after breathing it in during the entire bus trip. I'm almost dizzy as Papa and Mamma walk me deeper into the crowd.

Uniformed officers direct us in a steady stream of pedestrians like cattle being herded to the slaughter.

We pass under the Tobolskie Gate leading to the City Fortress. Once used to protect the citizens, it was then used to imprison them. The great Russian writer Fyodor Dostoevsky was once an unwilling guest. Walking into that stone fortress, hundreds of years old and the scene of so much misery, warfare and bloodshed, I feel like I am leaving the last vestiges of my old life, and of society itself, behind.

"Not a single one," I hear somebody say. I do not recognize the voice, low and gravelly but still remarkably loud; a threatening bark. "In all the Omsk, there is not one woman who will suffice for our needs, not a single one!"

Then the crowd parts, almost as if organized to do so, and it reveals him. We've never met, but I recognize him.

From my visions.

This is not the man with the heavy brow, pronounced like an ape's over his cold, lifeless eyes and adorned with scraggily eyebrows, like stretches of thorny thicket. I recognize the absence of his sneering smile, hatred the only thing that can inspire its mirth.

This is the other man; the sorrowful skeleton, the pale ghost of delusion.

I feel his eyes lock onto me, his words trailing off. When he shouts, "You there, hold!" my stomach turns, hairs on the back of my neck standing on end.

For he wasn't the only person in my vision that day. I was included, in agony, twisted and tortured, bruised and bleeding, filthy and denigrated.

I stop, Papa and Mamma standing nervously behind me as the man approaches, several uniformed KGB officers behind him. He approaches me slowly, looking me over. Even hunched forward, with my mother's worst clothes draped over me, his eyes find my hidden curves, the firmness of my youth, the fullness of my eyes and lips.

He says, "Who are you?"

Papa says, "I am Boris Zolotov. This is my wife and daughter. She is ill, we are just taking her to get some medical attention."

The KGB agent looks me over, his rough fingers pushing up under my chin to reveal my face more clearly to him. His breath collects between us in a cloud of herring and vodka.

He may have seemed sorrowful to me in my vision, but here he is all business, all power and authority and rigor and the things that makes an officer great but a man monstrous.

"What strikes you, child?" he asks me. "An ailment of the body, perhaps? Is there some congestion of the chest?" He let his eyes linger over me, sinking from my breasts as he added, "Perhaps you are in need of a detailed, physical examination."

"Please," Mamma says, "she is our only daughter!"

"So I presume," he says, his voice quick with an angry snap. "Otherwise you risk the State's wrath for not bringing both. Now hold your tongue, woman, lest I be forced to remove it and then hand it to you personally."

I clear my throat. "Forgive her, sir," I say, my voice lilting and meek, turning to my parents to say, "I do feel better now, just as you thought I might."

The man looks me over and nods, his thick lips pressing against each other in a satisfied grin. "I'm very glad to hear it," he says. "No reason the entire family should succumb to a single malady, eh?" After an ugly silence, echoing with his threats, he turns back to me and says, "Yevgeny Dragunov."

I bow my head. "Aleksandra, sir."

Agent Dragunov nodded again, as if pleased with my

subjugation. "You are quite lovely, Aleksandra. Do you know that?"

"Only if you say it is so, sir."

A tense silence passes, followed by a crackle of laughter as ugly as the face it bursts from. He says, "You lie splendidly, which proves you are as smart as you are beautiful."

He glances at my parents behind me, his voice taking a strict, authoritarian tone. "You have served your country well."

"Oh no," Mamma began to mutter, a sob welling up behind her aging face as her body sinks toward Papa's side, his arm wrapping around her.

Agent Dragunov says, "You are pleased to be able to serve the government in this way, I trust. You don't harbor any... subversive notions or other overtly... individualistic delusions?"

I can see Papa wrestling with himself, barely holding back from letting loose with the full brunt of his frustration and sorrow. "I... "

"Yes, comrade?"

Don't do it, Papa, I silently urge him, knowing he can understand me. I'm not the only one in the family with a brain especially tuned to things that other people cannot see or feel or hear or understand. It's one of the things that brought me and Papa so close to each other. I've always known that, in part at least, my visions reminded him of me and his own sensitivities.

Agent Dragunov stares at Papa and so do I, soon Dragunov's eyes go from Papa to me and back, as if he knows we can communicate on a different level, even if it only because we are father and daughter.

I will go with this man if I must, but only in the service of keeping you and Mamma alive. If you prefer, you can attack this man, cry out your anger and fear and sorrow and loss. I will join you, and the three of us will die together.

I can see my father reasoning it out. Life would not go on as before, there is no doubt about this anymore.

But it could still go on. And that meant one thing.

Papa lowers his head, bowing slightly to Agent Dragunov. "We are overcome with gratitude is all." My papa turns to look at me even as he addressed Dragunov. And I know the subtext of what he is saying, and I know who he is really addressing. "To serve in this way is a... a higher honor than I could have imagined. The joy I have known today will stay with me always."

Mama sobs harder, even as she fights back her misery and bites down on her tears.

I say, "Tell my brothers that I will always think kindly of them, and that I look forward to a time when we will all be together again."

Mamma smiles through her tears, but cannot stand the strain. She buries her face in Papa's side as he reaches down to stroke my cheek. "Sandra," he says, "the sun of my day, the star of my night."

Agent Dragunov glances at us again, taking in Papa's erstwhile bravery, Mamma's crumbling courage and my own grim determination that both of them get back on that bus and be returned safely to our home.

Their home.

Dragunov says to one of his officers, "Take her." The officer, a tall and burly man, steps casually over to me, extending his hand that I should follow him. With a last look back at my huddled and humbled parents, I nod and follow the officer, the image of my stooped and sobbing family etched into my mind. No horror the KGB can offer will hurt more, but this brings me no solace.

A second later, I turn again for a last glimpse of those two lovely and loving people, who bore and sired and raised me, who loved me and protected and nurtured me.

But they are already gone, swallowed up by the crowds of young women, their own parents, and the KGB menace that strolls among them.

I am the only young woman taken from Omsk that day, leaving behind what is certain to be a happy and relieved population, save for a tiny handful.

My family.

But I hold tight to their memory, their faces and the times we shared; the fights and the flights of fancy, the miseries and the meanings behind them. I tell myself I'll never forget them, and I don't doubt it for a moment.

I don't expect to live long enough to forget anything.

I sit in the bed of an army truck, canvas draped over its steel-ribbed frame. The ride is painful, every bump in the road shooting directly up through the balding tires and the rusted metal, through the wooden bench and into my posterior; the pain shooting up my spine to coil in my brain in a seething headache.

And the truck sways, squeaking shocks beneath us failing to hold the vehicle steady on the long highway to Novosibirsk.

Across from me, a young soldier sits with a rifle in his hands. He stares at me, his face a grim mask. I look around the otherwise-empty truck, realizing they'd intended to be bringing back a lot more women.

But I am the only one.

And with nobody else to look at, I draw my guard's undivided attention. His gray eyes crawled up and down my body, even under the layers of tattered, mildewed wool. When his eyes finally reach mine, a little smile curls into his left cheek, then sinks down again to resume his angry frown. His head is large, fleshy, jowls rippling slightly with the motion of the truck.

I try to look away, but I can feel his stare boring holes into the side of my head, and through my clothes to the vulnerable flesh within.

I know what he's thinking.

Who knew I'd be alone with just one woman? he contemplates. Nobody ever mentioned it, or anything like what I should or shouldn't be doing with the prisoners.

I can't help it, my eyes drifting toward him against my better judgment and against the straining and yearning of every muscle in my body. As soon as my gaze meets his again, it touches the spark that ignites the flame.

The guard puts his rifle aside and pulls open his belt buckle even as he is falling on top of me, three feet in front of him.

I reach out instinctively, my lips parting in a scream. The first suggestion of my call for help rattles around the truck bed until the guard's flattened hand falls down over my face, clamped over my mouth. My own hot breath bounces against my lips, from my nostrils to the side of his palm and back up, pushing the hair from my face as he looms over me, panting and grinning and grunting.

His smell overpowers me, the stench of his body odor having soaked into his ill-fitting woolen uniform. With his free hand, he reaches down to un-sheathe himself. His hips thrust forward and push my skirt up around my hips. I struggle, kicking at his hips and back with fruitless aggression. My left hand pulls at the hand he uses to gag me.

This leaves my right hand free.

In the cab, the driver and his guard may feel the commotion, they may feel the vibrations of the struggle, but I can't know if they understood them or if they even care to stop them.

My mind is alert, even in the frenzy of the attack, the panic of the assault as it changes the shape of my life forever, bending its course irreversibly into darker terrain. I've been in such terrain before, and I know the only ways out.

After Gregory found me in that field with the two minors, he showed me ways to quickly thwart an attacker, and those lessons come back to me like the quick rescue of my brother himself; action that feels alien to my own body, independent of my decisions or willingness. And it isn't about size, or strength.

It's about speed.

It's almost like I'm watching it all happen, even as I am in the center of the horror.

My right fingers clamp together, bending at the knuckles. The muscles along my arm clench, contracted before releasing their energy and springing out at my attacker. My knuckles find their mark, his fleshy jowl just below the jawbone. I can feel his windpipe collapse as my knuckles jab into his throat.

He looks at me in shock and pain, eyebrows high on his surprised expression, his beady eyes round beneath them. His body feels instantly heavier, dead weight on top of me, pushing my legs aside.

But my right hand isn't finished, because neither is he. But instead of my stiffened fingers bent at the knuckles, my hand bends back, presenting the ball of my palm.

But the same muscles pull my arm back, and then release it once more in a blur of bone and thrust, energy pouring from my arm and through my hand as it rams my guard's nose, sending the plank of cartilage there rushing into his skull and digging into his brain.

Blood shoots out of his nostrils, his nose a fleshy, sagging snout pushed and hanging down. His head back, I can push him off me. He falls to the floor of the bed of the truck, staring up as blood pours out of his face, rattling gurgles leaking up from his crippled windpipe.

He lays on his back, staring up, bloodied, his body quivering, fingers twitching.

He'll be dead soon.

I look at his army-issue rifle still leaning up against his side of the bed. I have two choices, neither of them promising at all. The first is to grab the rifle. I can start firing toward the cab at the front of the truck, enough shots roughly aimed to end the lives of the men in front.

But that would cause a crash, and in the center of an eight-truck convoy I know that if I manage to survive the crash, I won't escape the scene. As soon as I kill the driver, I'll be killing myself.

I can hold onto the rifle, aiming it at the rear entry to the truck bed. When whoever comes for me did so, I can open fire with everything the rifle has. There is a chance the convoy would break up and go to different locations. In that case, I could be alone with only two guards and then I'd be free to escape.

Or I could kill only two out of a dozen of more, and then my death would be certain.

And, I have to remind myself, they'll know it was me and they'll go back for my family.

The gulag.

No, I have to correct myself, *not anymore.* It's been the gulag for so long, the shadow of death hanging over our heads and stretching so tall and dark that it is hard to remember that they'd closed the gulag down the year before, in 1960.

Now there is the Ministry of Justition RF, now there are the institutions of the GUIN MVD Directorate of Corrections of Ministry of Justice.

Said to be even worse.

Which leaves a single choice; sit on that bench and watch the man die, leaving his rifle untouched. When the truck stops and they come for me, they'll see me unarmed and hopefully,

I won't be killed and I'll live on to escape at a better time.

I don't have confidence in any of the three options. But I don't have a fourth choice.

The truck rumbles around me and my dying guard, our bodies swaying and bobbing in a final dance of death, a slow waltz into the grave. Soon enough, I notice his chest ceases to heave, his throat goes silent.

Two hours after the man's death, the truck finally stops. I wait while the activity buzzes around the truck. I hear the cab doors opening and closing, footsteps of the driver and his guard and those of the others.

We're not alone, I realize. I'll never be able to shoot my way out of this.

But I don't have long to think about it, as the driver and his guard call for my guard a third time, increasing worry in their timing and tone.

Then they throw the canvas flap open at the rear of the truck cab, calling the man's name one last time. Shock takes their expressions, mouths small, jaws dropping, heads dipping forward.

I sit with my arms crossed in front of me, meek as I can appear. I know it's my only chance. And for some reason, men always respond to that coming from me; so it's a good chance too.

They look at me, and at my guard. One pulls his handgun on me and my blood runs cold. Nerves twitch, but I try not to move. My blood freezes, but I'm careful not to exhibit any reaction at all. Even the slightest movement can bring death to me, a death that happens so fast it would take me off the Earth before I even realize.

My heart pounds in my chest, my mouth filled with a foul flavor; the panicky taste of the grave. My lips stick together, suddenly dry. I can't swallow. Beads of sweat break out along the crevice of my spine, instantly chilling in the late-winter cool.

One of the guards puts his hand out to lower the other's gun, muttering and shaking his head. "We knew what he was up to back there," he says. "Yuri knew his luck wouldn't last."

They both glare at me, smiles stretching across their angular faces as little chuckles bubble up. The one lowers his gun and steps away from the exit of the truck bed.

One looks at me and says, "Miss?" very politely.

At first, my legs won't move.

Soon enough my reflexes kick in again and my body

manages to carry me onward, further from my treasured past and deeper into my mysterious future.

Novosibirsk's government center is filled with families, each including a young woman, just as Omsk has hosted.

More young women for the KGB.

But why? Surely, this amount of trouble and expense would never be put to the mere task of collecting whores or even sex slaves. Such women disappear from the streets all over Siberia and all of Russia, Europe, the United States, the Latin countries like Mexico and those in Central and South American. Young Russian and Siberian women are lining up to become whores just to escape to the west; the KGB wouldn't go to such trouble simply to coral and export these women. And we aren't spies, because the KGB isn't hunting us like spies.

I realize that we're part of a massive effort of some kind. Something big and sophisticated, like the KGB itself.

And something just as deadly.

I notice other trucks like the one that brought me. I notice other women like myself; young and strong or at least fit, and all pretty, peering out from the feeble disguise of worn and ugly peasant's garb.

We aren't fooling anyone but ourselves. And we share eye

contact in the same fleeting way that prisoners might, or even gladiatorial competitors; with understanding, solidarity.

And with a cold-blooded willingness to kill or be killed, even while hoping against hope that we wouldn't have to be killing each other.

But still knowing that it is more than likely.

Certainly, the leisure of choosing whom we might kill or whom might kill us will be out of our reach, at least initially.

But somebody will be killing somebody, which seems clear to everyone.

One young woman is a redhead, tall and striking, with high cheek bones and glaring blue eyes. She has suffered, I know in an instant. She walks with a tall woman of some mixed descent; she looks to have African and Asian blood, an exotic mix that in this case created a tall, muscular beauty of considerable influence and stamina. Another is a short brunette, powerful and muscular, anger pumping out of every pour, a sneer to match the grizzliest face from my ugliest vision.

Each woman is escorted by an armed guard.

Around us, other families mingle and murmur, worrying and wondering and hustling about in a mad dash to remain unseen; hiding in plain sight.

The clamor of the worried Siberians and the muddled, muffled questions from the specks of uniformed KGB officers rises around us as our guards lead us onto a train platform.

Agent Dragunov, whose face still resembled the hard mask of an officer and not the melancholy despair of my vision, paces in front of me and the three other women, all of whom are roughly my age.

"You have been brought here because you stood out," he says, pausing in front of me. His eyes dig into my soul, but they come up empty. "You have excellence," he adds, "and that is what Mother Russia needs, now more than ever. I know you have fear, because you are human and, of course, because you are women. But conquer your fear! You are not merely women, but women of Russian Siberia, and you will rise to the task the way a true Russian will always do, even one of your ... reduced gender."

The other women and I do not exchange knowing glances, raised brows and half-smiles of our own that say, Who does this idiot think he's kidding? Does he know where he or any of his fellow men would be without us women? Are men this dense the world over?

Are they this dangerous?

Dragunov resumes pacing in front of us, saying, "You will

transcend your roles and become tools of the State in ways you could never have imagined. If you mourn for yourselves or your families, I cannot discourage you. Mourn for yourselves, because your old selves are dead, and you are here to be born anew, true sucklings of the Russian Bear."

He stops pacing and talking. I hope he's finished with this lecture. It is beyond depressing; I'm sure they feel it is necessary, but mostly it just makes me wish for home more not less. "Mourn for your families," Dragunov resumes pacing and lecturing, "because you may not cross their paths again in this life. Instead, your paths will take you elsewhere, to where you never dreamed and from which you may not return. But you will have the honor of service beyond the others, a life beyond your limited foresight and opportunities for you and Mother Russia. It is your honor and your duty to make the most of these opportunities, and to make the most of yourselves and of the State. You will not deny Mother Russia, or yourselves or your destinies."

He stops in front of me again, my blood running cold with his icy stare. Something about the hollowness of his glare, the soullessness of it, frightens me to my very core. But I am not afraid of this man, so much as I am afraid of what has reduced him to this echoing shell of once-vital human being.

For now, he is more machine than man; and what manner of

man lies within the machine, I do not want to know.

But I feel that, once again, that choice will not be mine to make.

He says, "Your lives are no longer your own, in truth they never were. Our great nation was waiting to reap the harvest of her loins, and now..." He smiles at me before adding, "Now the fruit is ripe. The time for harvest has come."

The four of us are piled into a train car, empty but for some straw on the wood-plank floor, wreaking of animal waste. They slam the door shut, heavy and loud, creaking and croaking. We sit in the long, heavy darkness, light streaming in through the slats in the wooden sides of the train car. The silence is nearly deafening, the slightest cough or sneeze seeming to reverberate around the empty train car like a collapsing building.

There is so much I want to ask these women. *Why you? Why me? Why us? Why? And what, and for whom?* Well, I know for whom. For Mother Russia. And the other questions, they'd only ask me in return.

In Russia, one learns that silence is in many ways as telling as any words at any volume. The less one says, the more one can hear and understand and the less another can do the same. Silence heals and protects, it also assaults and thwarts and reduces an enemy into a disappeared memory or another ugly story to be told by the old women in the textile mills.

After what seems like hours, my legs are stiff and my feet burning but my body unwilling to sink to the filthy, damp floor. The door slides open with a sudden clamor and light spills in, nearly blinding me. I squint through my tightened eyelids, failing to focus on the bodies and faces of another dozen or so young women as they pile into the car.

The door slides shut again.

The silence among us gets even louder, the reverberation of unspoken words banging against the wooden planks and against the insides of my skull.

But there are no answers. Only time will provide them. And we have plenty of that.

For now.

After a few more hours, loud hisses surround the car, the slow grinding of the train's machinery beneath us jostling our tired bodies as the train begins crawling forward.

Toward Moscow.

Toward our destinies.

And there is no turning back.

CHAPTER THREE

"A man is known by the silence he keeps." -- Oliver Herford

April 1961

I drift off to sleep during the train ride to Moscow, my legs having finally given out after almost sixteen hours of standing up. When the train stops, amid the hissing of steam, greasy wheels slowing beneath the calming train car, I wake up not from the sudden movement but from the sudden *lack* of movement.

The doors pull open again and I have to squint in the burning sunlight, the glare bouncing off the snowy street and nearly blinding me.

A bus with metal grating on the windows is waiting to take us into the heart of the city.

Moscow.

I've never seen the great city before. Here it seems to be as they say, that life is without limits. We roll through modern streets, cars and brick buildings reflecting the modern hustle of our post-war world, everything sleek and slick and fast. We pass the Kremlin building in Red square, huge and ornate, and the Pokrovsky Cathedral, still as colorful and grand as it was when Ivan the Terrible had it built in the 1500s.

What city ever intermingled the old and the new with such aplomb? I wonder. The Nazi's recent reign of terror had wiped out a lot of Europe's medieval cities. But Hitler never got to Moscow, so it remains complete in its historical aspect, protected by the very isolation which may ultimately be its undoing.

But they do say that the world seems to be getting smaller and smaller, and even as my own world tumbles in an interlocking of contraction and expansion, somewhere between everything out there and nothing at all, I know that the old saying is true. With television becoming so popular, air travel so common, it won't be long before the iron grip of the Kremlin rusts and rots and dissolves and the Russian people run mad with glee in the streets, free to come and go as they please.

Free.

But that isn't the case yet. There is still so much fear and hatred of the West, especially the United States, Moscow will remain cloistered, secluded, protected.

Safe.

But not free.

The bus pulls up to the KGB headquarters in Lubyanka Square. The huge building is a massive brown box, eight stories or more of tan brick and gold trim, the first level a flat gray. Windows punctuate the facade, bringing light into those lucky enough to inhabit one of the offices above the main floor. I know instinctively that the basement floors are where the real horrors of this place occur, and that's where we women will be going.

Indeed, the bus pulls into a subterranean parking garage and then down several levels. Several uniformed KGB officers usher us out of the bus and into the garage, our footsteps and the metal clanks of the rifles echoing in the cold, dark, concrete cavern.

I look around and wonder if I'll ever see sunlight again.

Double doors are pushed open in front of us, long hallways await, lit by small bulbs affixed to the walls at fifteen-foot intervals.

Nobody speaks, not because we all know it would not be allowed. There's simply nothing more to say.

We are led into a large room, where several small chairs with attached desks sit lined up in rows, facing front, like a classroom. We are lined up facing the chairs, only ghosts inhabit them now, of children long grown up or dead.

I stiffen as the two guards do, turning to the door as a familiar man enters. He's not familiar because I've met him before. I haven't. But I've seen his face in my visions.

He approaches us slowly, his pronounced ridge low over his eyes, his gnarled brows tangled over his lifeless eyes, thick lips slick with his own saliva. The creases on his thick, leathery skin bely his age, at least fifty. His body is bulky, graceless as he paces in front of us.

"I am Division Commander Alexei Vasilyevich Sobchak," he says, his voice low and gravelly, filled with phlegm. "From this point forward, everything in your lives, and your lives themselves, are in my hands. You will look upon me as the State itself; undeniable, inescapable, indomitable."

He stops to glare at me, in the center of the line.

"You are here to serve Mother Russia. As you serve me, so shall you be serving her." He peers into my eyes, but I stare straight ahead, trying my best to look past him, to look through him. He considers as he glares at me, but I can't be sure what he's thinking. I half-wonder if he can hear my heart beating faster, or sense the dread that wells up inside me with his nearness. He smiles and moves on down the line.

Yes, I realize, he can.

He says, "If you do as you are told, you will have the honor of serving our country for many years, and in strength and good health. If you fail or rebel, your lives will end quickly and without exception. Your families already consider you to be dead."

One of the girls brakes out in a gasp at this harsh truth. We all know it and think it in our protracted silence, but the stress and the reality finally cracks her solemn facade with a panicked release.

Sobchak turns and slaps her hard across the face, her black hair falling forward as her body snaps to the side.

"Strength is what the Kremlin needs, you simpering fool! Now get a hold of yourself," he turns to us to add, "all of you! Weakness will not be tolerated."

Sobchak turns to one of the guards and nods. The guard nods back and opens the door. Sobchak exits, his gait stiff and strong, and the guards lead us out behind him, into the hallway and down the other direction.

We are put into rooms, furnished only with bunk beds and

dressers already filled with gray wool garments of only two kinds; pants and shirt.

I am paired with the tall, striking redhead they'd picked up in Novosibirsk. We stand for a minute, looking around the silent sequestration of our new home.

Told to say nothing to the women we are paired with, I can't help but extend my hand to her and say, "I'm Aleksandra."

"Ivanna," she says, glaring at my hand and not shaking it. I lower my rejected palm back to my side and sit down on the thin mattress, springs squeaking beneath me. Several hours later we are taken to a mess hall to rejoin the other women, a plate of mashed oats and water and a raw beet presented to each of us. It's the first meal I've had in over twenty-four hours, but it still tastes like wet cardboard and, well, a beet.

We're brought back to our rooms and the lights are turned off automatically.

My sleep is filled with visions; Papa and Mamma sitting quietly; she from exhaustion and he from abject misery, the little house dimly lit around them to match their internal gloom.

I see the sad-faced KGB officer again, who'd introduced himself as Dragunov, his sorrow still overtaken by his officiousness.

I see another man's face, not Dragunov or Sobchak or Papa, not Gregory or Vlad or any of the men I knew in the Omsk. He's handsome, smiling casually, hair graying slightly. My knight in shining armor come to rescue me? I feel his warm arms wrapping me in their protection I love this man; vision of my dreams. I will meet him one day, I hope. If I can survive Mother Russia.

In my mind's eye, he gently pulls my chin up so that my lips are angled toward his, and he leans in and kisses me. It sends a chill through me, and I feel a slight wetness between my legs. I have dreamt of this man since my childhood; a combination of my gentle giant of a father and a beautiful fantasy man with pretty green eyes, blondish, brown hair, tall, strong, tanned and muscular. In that moment, I forget where I am, then clanging doors and sudden darkness brings me back to my harsh reality. I will probably never meet my fantasy man. I will, more than likely, die an agonizing death at the hands of some torture mad administrator in the heart of the Kremlin.

***

The next day, our training begins. We sit in the big classroom we'd been brought to before, each in a small chair-and-desk, paper and pencils in front of us. Dragunov himself stands at the head of the class, several words written in chalk on the blackboard: *nouns, verbs, adjectives.*

The words are written in English.

The hours crawl by, turning slowly into days as Dragunov drills the lessons into us. *Cat. Dog. May I have a glass of water?*

He approaches my roommate Ivanna, leaning over her. "Where is the restaurant?"

Ivanna answers, "The restaurant is down the street."

After a tense silence, Dragunov nods and turns to another young woman, the brunette who'd gasped in line before. He says, "What is the name of your dog?"

She sits there, uncertain, looking around as if the answer is written on the walls.

It isn't.

Dragunov repeats, "What is the name of your dog?" even louder.

Finally, she answers, "The name of my dog, it is... hamburger."

"No!" Dragunov screams, slapping the poor brunette again. But she's not the only one. Over the course of our first week, nobody escapes the wrath of Dragunov's hand.

"It is only English," Dragunov screams at us, "the language of the miserable and the damned. If you are to be any more than that, you must master this foul tongue, or have your own cut out of you."

We learn fast.

And English isn't the only subject of study. At night we are instructed by KomDiv Sobchak himself, sometimes a less brutal man called Kubichek who seems sad and in constant mourning. *Does he mourn for us?" Does he know that I am headed for my death?* His approach is gentle, persuading and persistent.

"You must try harder, Aleksandra," He whispers this in my ear one evening when it is just me, the other women and him. "You have the best chance of all of these women to survive the training, but you must try harder." He continues away down the aisle drilling everyone. *Why did he tell me that? Survive this?* Up until now, we haven't been told what our progress meant.

In a few minutes, Kubichek is dismissed by KomDiv Sobchak who comes in pacing and continues to pace up front and roving the aisles like a tiger searching for prey. "To properly control a person's mind," Sobchak says, "you must know their values, their emotions and desires and beliefs. These are their weak points, the best places of successful attack. Most important are the values, as they instruct what the subject wants, what motivates them to do the thing which you want them to do."

Mind control, I say to myself. English and mind control. Why? But it can only be one thing. I must work harder, try harder to stay alive.

Spying, I realize. On the British? No.

On the Americans.

"You must appeal to your subject's identity and ego," Sobchak says, strolling down the aisle next to my chair. "Such as..." I look up and he stares down at me, thick lips in an expectant frown.

In English, I say, "You... you are a fine person, honest..."

Sobchak stares at me, then nods and turns to the others, his voice bouncing off the walls. "That is correct!" His fat fingers roll on the little desktop in front of me, his only acknowledgement to me directly before moving on.

He snarls at another woman, a smaller redhead with freckled skin and frightened blue eyes. She could be Ivanna's sister. He says to her, "Impress me."

She looks around, uncertain, and says, "You... you are a fine person, honest..."

Sobchak sits in the nervous tension that follows as if savoring it, nodding as if agreeing on some fine point, but only with himself. He screams out, "Stupid cow!" before striking her hard across the face. She falls out of her chair and lays on the floor, crumpled and cowering and sobbing into her hands. His face is screwed up in disgust. "I will show you how I teach stupid cows who can't impress me." He kicks at her, nudging her with his boot. "Get up, cow."

"Please KomDiv Sobchak, I can do better." The woman gets to her feet, now pleading, wringing her hands, tears streaming down her face. I know that is a mistake. If there's one thing I've learned since coming here is that weakness is not tolerated. Pleading definitely falls into that category.

"Guards!" Sobchak turns away from her, his nose screwed up in a look of disgust. He looks like somebody had defecated in front of him. Two armed men enter from the hallway, eager and ready as they always appear to me. I think they like their job. "This one needs to be retrained."

"No," she says, increasing horror in her expression as the volume rises in her throat. "Please, no!" *Mistake. Shut up.* I will her silently to hold her tongue. *Doesn't she remember Tatiana? She screamed and hollered when she left, and she never came back.*

The guards pick her up, one by each arm, and drag her out of the room. She begins to kick and struggle, pulling away but unable to escape their grip as they carry her out of the room, her screams fading down the hall with her. *One less woman to beat*. I know this place is changing me. I never would have thought that at home.

But, this isn't home. I'll never see home again.

Terrible silence returns to the class room, nervous glances being exchanged. Ivanna and I share one such look, the dread we both feel for our classmate matched only by the dread we feel for each other, and ourselves.

It could be any one of us.

Clearing his throat, Sobchak continues as if nothing has happened, "Hypnosis is another matter altogether..."

***

January 1962

It feels like years, but in actuality, it's only been some months since we arrived at this place. We follow the same routine, day and night, night and day. Sobchak, Kibiechk, Dragunov, Sobchak again On and on, drill, drill, drill.

Impress me. I hate those words. Impress me or disappear

and most probably die.

Sobchak says, "In order to get somebody to believe they will benefit from doing what you want them to do, you must always consider the *do you know* technique. Ask your subject to imagine what other thing might provide the benefits which the action you suggest will provide. Examples?" He turns to me. "Aleksandra?"

I don't have to think about it long. Like a childhood riddle or the rudimentary concept behind the Russian doll, this is no great mystery to me. I'm not sure why I grasp these concepts so readily, but I do.

I say, "Can you imagine what other technique will more readily help you to manipulate your subject and accomplish your goal?"

After a brief silence, Sobchak barks out an angry laugh, enjoying my cleverness and my stubbornness.

He turns to the meek brunette. "Example."

The brunette says, "Can you imagine ... what other secrets there are to share?"

Sobchak shakes his head, eyes rolling in his wide skull. He draws back his fist, ready to smash her pretty face in yet again, until a single voice in the room shocks everybody into stillness, including me.

Even though the voice is my own.

"Get away from her!"

All eyes turn to me. *What have I done?*

Sobchak looks at me, his hand sinking slowly to his side. "What did you say, girl?"

It's too late to deny it, and though I think I probably could dismantle Sobchak in front of the other women, I know I'll be killed as soon as Sobchak finishes making a bloodied example out of me; and that would be a painful, protracted example indeed.

Instead I can only sit in the stillness of guilt and await the terrible ramifications.

I don't have to wait long.

Sobchak's hand cuts through the air with a whoosh and strikes the right side of my face like an iron hammer. Pain rings in my skull, banging through my brain and back again, eyeballs rattling in their sockets. I feel my body snap to the side but right itself instantaneously. Instead of a sob, my mouth turns in a tense smile, lips pulled tight over my clenched teeth. Instead of facing downward or crying into my hands, I am facing him again before I know it, before I have to time to consciously decide otherwise.

He detests weakness. I detest him.

He stares down at me and I stare up at him, the tension in the room so thick it may smother us all. His face becomes red, head quivering with his confused rage. He calls, "Guards!" and they enter while is voice is still reverberating around the room. "This one!"

I don't resist. I follow the uniformed thugs, each with their fingers digging unnecessarily into my arms. I don't look back with desperation; I don't scream or plead; I look forward and walk head-long into the nightmare that I know awaits me.

They take me to a room below the one we all inhabit, which is at least two stories below the street. I imagine one layer below lay the Christian's hell.

I'm already stepping into a personal hell of my very own.

They pull the gray pants and shirt off me and chain my wrists to manacles that hang from a metal hook drilled into the ceiling. My muscles stretch, my arms pressing against the sides of my neck, chest pulled tight, my naked breasts hanging vulnerable in front of me.

In the corner is a boy, battered, naked about 10 years old.

He doesn't look at me, but I can see the back of him is bloody. *What did they do to you, boy? What will they do to me?*

The guards leer at me, nodding to each other and muttering, eyes tracking the lines of my bare flanks, the graceful thighs, my blonde hair pouring past my creamy shoulders.

They see me as sexual, now more than ever, and I know it. And they know it too.

But for whatever reason, I am left alone in that room, untouched by their lusty hunger.

Orders, I realize. *His orders*. Because he wants me for himself.

Then let him come, I say to myself, recognizing my dear brother's words in my own inner voice. *This wolf will get as much as he can handle.*

"Hey, boy." I whisper in the child's direction. He doesn't respond just continues to cower in the corner, eyes wide open, mouth apart. I think he's drooling. "Hey, can you hear me?" A lost cause. Whatever they'd done to him, his mind appeared to be gone.

The hours crawl by, my arms stinging with pain from the sheer lack of movement, blood unable to keep rushing upward into my swollen, purple hands, fingers long since gone numb.

It's hard to breathe now, my ribs pressing against my lungs, my arms pressing against my windpipe.

My own tired voice creeps up out of my throat, the last of my strength beginning to seep away.

Then the door opens and closes behind me.

"Hello, Aleksandra."

I don't need to crane my head for a better look behind me. I recognize that bastard Sobchak's voice, and the drunkenness of his slurred greeting. He's finished with the class, treated himself to some vodka, and now he's come for me.

Good, I say to myself. Let him get close enough to kick his balls in, give him something to remember me by.

No, I tell myself. Hold back. Be smart, remember what they're teaching upstairs. Once you lose control, you won't be able to get it back.

I watch him walk towards the child appearing to be about to pat him on the head. The boy skitters closer to the wall trying to blend in. "Get me hard." He opens his pants, I hear, his back mostly towards me. I hear the child gagging, crying. "Good boy. You do yum-yum so good." Sobchak's hips are moving back and forth as he pushes his shaft in and out of the child's mouth. "Oh, that feels so good. Yum-yum, good, feels so

ROBERT FURST & ALAN PARKER

good."

From his voice, I can tell Sobchak is drunk. After a few more thrusts, he stops and turns his attention to me. I watch as he steps in front of me, his shirt already off to reveal his bulky, hairy body, chunks of muscle and gobs of fat in different spots of his torso, giving him an oddly misshapen but no less intimidating appearance. His manhood is hard, sticking straight out in front of me. "Now for you, my dear Aleksandra." He spins me away from him, pulls on the chain to give me a bit more give, enough for me to bend over. I know where he plans to push his shaft next, and I vomit at the prospect.

He holds a bottle of vodka in his hand and takes another deep swig of it, swaying on his feet. I feel him looking at me, his drunken breath on my back. I imagine those dead eyes staring at me like he's done in countless classes before.

He stands me up, pulling hard on the chain that binds me. *Maybe, he's changed his mind.* I am grateful to be standing but my arms are numb and useless. "You," he gurgles, "you think you're so special. Daddy's little girl, I'll bet."

I don't answer, but my expression is cold and humorless and, most importantly, fearless.

He reaches up, the fingers of his free hand wrapping around my neck, squeezing hard. The pressure against my already-strained windpipe is almost too much, the collapse of my throat just an ounce of strength away; a bit more of his or a bit less of mine.

The outcome would be the same.

But my hands are bound above me, and I cannot feel them in any case. I know I can still kick him, and I count the seconds until that is my defense of last resort. He stares at me and I back at him, our wills locked together like the horns of two ram. His face grows red, and mine redder.

I know I am dying.

So, I pull up as much phlegm as I can, push it past his digging fingertips to the back of my tongue, and spit it with as much force as I can muster into his monstrous, pugged face.

The glob of phlegm covers parts of one cheek, his nose, one eye and his forehead. He winces in disgust and turns away for a moment, his eyes returning to mine as we stare each other down.

I've hit him with everything I have, and he is still squeezing. My lungs churn, struggling to pull in some life-giving air, enough at least to keep my heart beating a few moments longer. Blood runs in hot and then cold waves, my veins tingling as if ready to burst.

Even as my body shuts down, my brain flutters in what may be its final moments, its final visions.

I see familiar flashes of the man I now recognize to be Sobchak, in a room I now recognize as the one I'm in. I see myself, as I appeared in my previous visions and I as I appear now; grimy and naked and about to die.

I see others, women and men; the little redhead from my group, others that neither I nor anyone will ever see on this Earth again. I see their screaming, childlike faces. I see them writhe in pain under the sting of a whip. I seem them pulling and wrenching for a freedom they cannot win. I see him relishing their torment, savoring their terror and agony.

I see him standing behind them, bodies jittering from the very manacles that now bind me. I see him standing in front of a captive, pounding his naked pelvis into his prisoner's. I see their slim and naked bodies, male and female alike, lying in crumpled heaps on this very floor as Sobchak stands over them, satisfying his thirst for liquor to match his already-sated thirst for the carnal pleasures of unwilling young boys and unlucky young women.

I see him laughing and guzzling from that clear glass bottle, the vodka pouring into him to fuel his rage, his skin already sheeted in the sweat of his forcible coitus.

And, then I see my fantasy man, hands out, smile on his face, blue eyes twinkling. I hear him say, "I love you, Lexy." He is speaking English, American English. I am sad, because I know I will never meet him. I will never be loved by him, and I will never see my family or my home again.

Then Sobchak lets go, pushing me slightly as he backs up with a wicked chuckle. He puffs out his chest, arms slack at his sides. "Do you not fear the beast?" he challenges me, laughing at his own absurd presentation of man and monster. "All must cower before the beast, or be consumed by it!"

My voice is raspy, pushing out from my beleaguered throat. "I fear no man," I managed to say, "nor beast."

"Then the beast must destroy you!"

"No," I spit back, "the beast cannot destroy me. Because the beast knows I alone can do its bidding. And the beast knows that if I am tortured, if I am raped and defiled and battered, I will not be so well able to serve the beast or the State." I know it is a bold statement, a daring gambit that might end me or save me.

Sobchak stares at me, his expression dumbfounded as he sways, his belly reaching over the front of his pants.

"Even the beast must serve the State," I say. "The beast may be an animal, but it isn't a *stupid* animal."

Sobchak lurches at me, but stops himself even as I lean back on my chains, bracing for the worst.

When it doesn't come, I know I've found my enemy's weak spot. I say, "Like all animals, the beast respects strength; the beast wants to be tamed."

He takes another long pull from the bottle, each gulp only working to dull his senses and make him easier to manipulate.

"The beast is an animal and an animal does as it's told!" After a brittle silence passes, I say with rising anger and impatience, "Now release me, beast! Do as you're told! Obey me, you dumb brute, I order you!"

He stares at me for a minute and I almost think he's going to comply.

Then he sets the bottle down and unbuckles his pants.

"I'll show you the beast," he says.

And I know what he means; at least I think I do. But instead of pulling down his pants, he clutches the buckle, pulls the belt out and wraps it twice around his fist. He pulls it back and then strikes me with it across my exposed belly.

The pain shoots through me; up my spine and down my legs, my knees buckling. Another strike from the other direction hits me in the same place, just below the ribs on the taught flesh of my torso. Pain bursts out of my mouth in a clenched grunt, too powerful for me to withhold.

"I'll show you the beast!" he yells again, his voice more like a roar than a bellow. And he keeps roaring, a wordless battle cry as he brings that leather belt down onto me time and again. My thighs tremble with the sting of the blow, my ribs feet like they are cracking with the force and the energy from that speeding, flat leather ribbon. The sound alone, the smack of it against my numbing skin, is almost enough to make me vomit and I know that, if nothing else, I'll probably just choke to death in the process and at least this rain of anguish will be over.

At long last, no more pain.

A few more strikes of the whip and Sobchak backs off, weaving and leaning, breath panting in his heaving chest.

"The beast knows no master," he says, drunkenness overtaking him. He staggers up to me, reaching to open his pants and let them fall to his knees. He takes one step toward me and trips, falling forward with a grunt. He groans and gurgles, face-down on the floor, a few muttered words replaced by a loud, ugly snore.

The guards enter behind me. "KomDiv Sobchak!" They rush to pick him up, wincing from the alcohol vapors and struggling to lift his massive, dead weight. "Let's get him to bed."

I pass out while still hanging from the hook, but I wake up the next morning in my bed, my body racked with pain, my arms barely able to move. Ivanna silently helps me dress.

"We must not be late for class," she whispers, helping me to stand. Apparently, my return has lifted me in her esteem. Or, she just doesn't want to get in trouble for leaving me behind in bed. She carries my books and hers and we slowly ease our way to the classroom.

When Dragunov sees me an hour after I wake up, he knows where and vaguely how I spent my night. He looks almost sympathetic, but only for a moment. The hard mask of Soviet teacher and master crashes back down and his face is unreadable once more. Had he experienced the re-education chamber before? Was he once that little boy on the floor, brown curly hair, hunted gaze, terrorized gaze that looked almost animal. How had he come back from that world of insanity to become the man that he is? I am returned to the activity center leaving no room for further reflection.

***

August 1961

Our routine never changes. We sleep for eight hours and awake at six in the morning. We are fed and instructed in English, given an hour in the courtyard where we are exercised like horses in a pen, walking in slow laps. After our evening feeding, we begin mind control studies with Sobchak and, if we're lucky, we are returned to our quarters. Those who aren't fortunate are dragged to Sobchak's private torture room downstairs.

Every other day we are taken to communal showers where, under the watchful eyes of the guards, we strip and shower before being returned to our rooms.

Ivanna and I sit in the terrible stillness of our room, our eyes saying to one another what our lips cannot. We know these walls have ears, as well as teeth and claws.

The great Russian Bear is all around us.

They're training us to be spies, my glance tells Ivanna. Her nod tells me that she agrees.

Not all of us will make it.

Her grave expression offers her further agreement.

What will happen to the others?

We look at each other, both knowing the sad answer.

How many do they need or want? Must there be only one? How long before we are pitted against one another to make that sad determination?

Ivanna looks back at me. *I don't know. Soon.*

The door swings open, our heads turning to see two uniformed officers glaring at me. With just a jut of their heads, they instruct me to follow them out the door. Ivanna gives me a look of grim sympathy, not expecting me to return.

Goodbye, my friend, her look seems to be saying.

Good luck, I silently offer her in return.

They lead me down three halls and into an elevator. My guards, younger men but very tall and strong, stare straight ahead, their gazes never lingering over my body. I have the feeling they are ordered to behave this way, but I can only guess the reason.

Moments later I'm escorted into a private office where KGB Agent Yevgeny Dragunov himself stands waiting. I have become accustomed to seeing him every day in our English language study classes, but to see him in a different room, a small and private room, and also late at night; I know right away that teaching me English is the last thing on his mind.

He pours himself vodka, looking at me as he tips the decanter. I shake my head with a polite smile. He pours the drink anyway, and brings it to me.

"Thank you, Agent Dragunov."

"Please," he says, "call me Yev."

I take it as he guides me toward a chair on the opposite side of the desk. I sit as he clinks his shot glass to mine and drinks his vodka down in a single, swift pull. Looking at him, and then down at my own glass, I do the same. It burns as it goes down, but the rush of pleasure is a relief to my system.

I haven't known pleasure in so long I can barely remember ever having experienced it at all. Then I remember the endless days of playing and dancing among the wildflowers during the summers and in the winter snow. I remember nights by the fireplace with Papa, reading me *Peter and the Wolf* and my other favorite stories.

The pleasure of those memories brings back the sharp pain of their recent loss, the drastic change my life has taken.

I refocus on my surroundings, all pleasure fleeing once more.

Dragunov says, "You have done quite well, Aleksandra. KomDiv Sobchak and I agree, you have a promising future in the service of the State."

In English, I say, "You are too kind, sir."

At this, Dragunov breaks out laughing and shaking his head. Pouring himself another vodka, he brings me the decanter and refills my shot glass. "Very well indeed," he says to me, also in English.

I nod to acknowledge his return of my reference. The vodka trickles against the glass as the surface level rises to the top.

Dragunov says in our native Russian, "But your duties will go beyond merely speaking decadent English, beyond even the control of the mind which you've also been studying with great success."

I nod again. To say nothing is to ensure that I do not say the wrong thing, which can be lethal even under the best of circumstances.

And these are not the best of circumstances.

"You will have to control the body as well as the mind," Dragunov says, returning the decanter to the bar and raising his refilled glass. He smiles and drinks the vodka down.

He approaches me, pointing at the filled glass in my hand. "Drink up, Aleksandra," he says.

So I do.

I must.

Appeased, he says, "I see you've had drink before. And I've heard about what happened with you and your guard in the truck from Omsk City. You killed him with your bare hands, I'm told."

I turn my gaze downward, not wanting to challenge him and certainly not wanting to begin excusing myself or otherwise admitting anything.

He says, "Don't worry, you'll not be reprimanded. It speaks well of your qualifications. But it does lead us to wonder what experiences you might have with men beyond merely defending yourself from them?"

He reaches down and touches my chin, pulling my face up to meet his gaze. He smiles. "But how to qualify such a query?" he asks. "How best to... measure your intimate skills, the breadth of your seductive capabilities?"

I do not want to endure the answer to his rhetorical questions, any more than I did with the guard in the truck, the boys in the field or any other man of that temperament. I want to give myself up, not to be taken.

I flash back to the things we've been studying in the

evenings, wondering in that quicksilver light of inspiration how effective the tools would really be and knowing in that instant that I am about to find out.

I say, "I am so gratified that both you and the Komdiv are pleased. I appreciate his dedication and attention during our classes."

Dragunov turns his head slightly, as if to hear me better but in truth it is to understand me more clearly. "Have you... met privately with KomDiv Sobchak?"

Doubt, I remind myself. The best way to influence the subconscious mind.

I say, "I half-expected the Komdiv himself to be standing on the other side of this door."

Dragunov considers, eyes peering into some reasoning distance as he evaluates and then re-evaluates his position.

"But I'm sure that he would have no objection to you calling me in for a private meeting such as this one."

Dragunov's face goes pale.

I add, "And so what if he does? You have no fear of such a man, even if he is your so-called superior."

"Hold your tongue, woman," he says, lips pulled tight over his teeth.

"Let him think and do as he pleases. This is *our* time together, Yev -- "

"Agent Dragunov -- "

"-- And I'm so glad for it! I hoped you felt as I do. Whatever happens, even if that ugly old fool puts us both up in front of a firing squad, it will be worth it."

Dragunov calls, "Guards!"

But I ignore him. "Take me, Yev, take me and let them bury us together if they must!"

Even louder: "Guards!"

The office door flies open behind me and the guards step in, clutching their rifles. Dragunov says to them, "Take this woman back to her room, at once."

I shoot him a look of confusion and frustration, eyebrows high on my creased forehead, lips a sad little pout as they pull me out of the room.

I keep up the act until they shove me back into the room I share with Ivanna in soft whispers, who smiles, pleasantly surprised to see me. In our privacy, I can finally let my own smile break across my mask of faux disappointment.

At least the mind control works, my smile tells Ivanna.

Her nod tells me that she understands.

Although Sobchak brings me back for several more sessions under the ceiling hook, I am never approached by the coward Dragunov again. I often think that if Dragunov sees the burns and welts left on me by the beast's whipping, and the electrical shocks from the opened wires, and the purple bruises from the closed-fist punches he delivered to my ribs and belly, Dragunov probably wouldn't want me anymore anyway.

CHAPTER FOUR

"I became insane, with long intervals of horrible sanity". --
Edgar Allan Poe

October 1962

We've been training for several months, and one morning Ivanna and I are led into our classroom with only one other woman, the one of mixed descent, African and Asian.

We stand quietly in front of the desk, KomDiv Sobchak sitting behind it and Agent Dragunov standing beside him and one step behind. The two armed guards stand behind us as we face Sobchak and Dragunov.

Sobchak says, "Congratulations, ladies, you three have been selected to compete for an assignment with the KGB. Your performances in classes and on examinations have qualified you for this trial of your skills."

I stand, hoping my nerves aren't showing even as I feel my limbs shake. Months of doubt and speculation have led me to this moment of truth. A period of study can be trying, but a time of testing can be fatal. However, I survived to take the test. Now I am to learn the fate of those who failed, and I might yet join their sorrowful ranks.

Sobchak says, "The twelve women from your group have been divided into three groups of four women each, and they have been turned over to various police lockups around Moscow as being subversive American students. Their part in this trial is to maintain that charade. You will each pose as an American diplomat, sent to win their release. You will be given credentials, as the officers holding these prisoners have no idea of the true nature of these circumstances."

Agent Dragunov pulls three manila envelopes from the desk drawer and hands one to each of us.

Sobchak says, "Whomever among you can win the release of your four prisoners will qualify for the assignment. If more than one succeeds, our choice will be made by private deliberation."

Agent Dragunov says to us, "If you succeed, your four prisoners will be returned to their families. If you fail, they will be sent to the GUIN."

"And you will join them," Sobchak adds with a wet-lipped grin.

I stand there next to Ivanna. We both know the odds of us both returning successfully from this mission are slim to none; the odds are greater, in fact, that neither of us will come back at all.

But we don't dare glance at each other, for fear of how it will be interpreted.

Dragunov says, "Appropriate attire has already been put in your rooms, as well as personal effects befitting the roles you will be assuming. Good luck."

The guards open the doors and escort us out of the office and into a future that seems to promise unending misery in the Russian penal system.

Ivanna and I dress in silence, collecting our jewelry and the briefcase we are each given to affect the look of an American diplomat. Our gray skirts and jackets give us a look neither has evoked here before; sophisticated, classy.

Sexy. Powerful.

Primed and ready for the slaughter.

The door opens and we exchange a farewell glance. I take a

single step toward her and we hug, each with one arm around the other. But the guards grunt and jut their heads toward the door, and we know there is no more time for sentiment.

There is precious little time for anything.

We each get into the backseat of a different car and pull out of the subterranean parking lot. This is my first time out of the KGB building since entering it, and the sunlight streams through the clouds and into the car window, warming my face. I know what awaits me, my stomach churning with nervous bile. But the sunlight coaxes a smile out of my face anyway, perhaps the last one I'll ever enjoy.

My car pulls to a stop in front of a large stone building, one of the many police lockups around Moscow. My driver escorts me, dressed in his KGB uniform. I'm not sure why, but I believe he is intended to serve as a local escort, which I presume a diplomat would probably have, especially a young female such as myself.

I assume the role of agitated and determined American diplomat before entering the building, taking the front steps with aggressive assertiveness, feeling the ire swelling behind my breast as I pull the glass door open and step into the chaos of the police station.

My driver steps forward, saying in Russian, "I have a

diplomat here, from the American embassy."

I say to him, "I'll speak for myself, thank you very much." I turn to the officer behind the desk and say, "The four American students you're holding, where are they?"

The officer behind the desk glares at me, and then picks up a phone.

Moments later my KGB escort and I are in the private office of IVS coordinator Lt. Anton Bagirli, his skin-bald head reflecting the light from his desk lamp.

I say, in Russian, "The American government will not allow you to incarcerate these students. They're innocent of any intention to harm the State in any way."

Bagirli looks over my credentials, then glares up at me. "You're American? Your Russian accent is perfect. How long have you studied?"

I smile and nod to accept his interrogation as a compliment. In English, I say, "My whole damn life, buddy. Now let's talk about the international incident you're about to ignite if you send those little fillies up the river."

Bagirli says, also in English, "These women cannot prove their innocence. Whether they are a danger to the State is unknown."

I cross my legs and say, "Let's take a look at what *is* known, shall we? You could wrongfully arrest these women, and bring down a world-wide media storm. These aren't Sacco and Vanzetti, but four beautiful young American women. Tie them to the tracks and you'll be playing the villain for sure. You know how tense things are out there, here and in the West. Do you really think this is the time for an international showdown? Do you really want to be the one holding the bag when all this comes crashing down on you, which it will in about twenty-four hours if I don't arrive at the embassy with those women in tow; do you?"

Bagirli looks up at me, mouth a still slit, no sign of his inclination on his immobile expression.

"On the other hand," I add, "you can do the right thing and release four young women back to their native country and correct a huge injustice. You'll be avoiding an international incident, and isn't keeping the peace more or less what you're supposed to be doing?"

I can tell he's considering it. But like a lot of Russians, fear is motivating him toward inaction.

And for me, that means failure.

And life in prison.

I realize I have to press my position while I still have momentum. "Uncle Joe's dead, Lieutenant. You don't have anything to be afraid of. Hell, the longer they're here, the more complicated things are likely to get. As of now, you could turn them over to me and deny they were ever here to begin with, there will be no risk to you at all. But fail to hand them over to me now before word gets around and you lose the option. Then you'll be committed, and no matter how ugly things get, it'll be too late to stop it. That would be a show of weakness, something we both know you can't afford."

"It is already too late."

"It isn't and you know it," I say, my voice snapping with impatience. "But it will be soon. Lock those women up and you'll be locking yourself up with them. Raise the bayonet to them, you'll only be cutting your own throat." I can sense his doubt; I can hear the wheels churning under that bald pate.

I add, "Uncle Joe may be dead, but Uncle Sam sure ain't." I let a little smile punctuate my sentiment, the silence in the room my only ovation.

It takes two hours for Bagirli to make the necessary phone calls and to have the women processed out of the IVS. My KGB agent makes a call or two in this time as well, leaving me to sit and ponder how dangerously close I'd come to falling into the bottomless pit of the Russian penal system, a living

79

hell.

But I didn't. Not only did I not fall in, but I saved four others from doing so; four women whose relief must be beyond measure.

Four families can now share that relief.

But not mine.

I know I have succeeded, but I'm still tense. Until I get out of this building with my four charges safely delivered, I won't be safe and I will not relax. I know things can change at any moment. A phone call from the KGB could still upend my entire campaign. And the reasons they might have for doing such a thing could be endless, beyond my imagining. However hard I flail, however well my efforts are applied, I know I am at the whimsy of much greater forces, and that they can tear me apart at will.

My KGB escort and I are finally reunited with the four women, the gasping brunette among them. We quietly walk out of the building and to our car, a second one parked behind it and waiting.

The brunette smiles at me and whispers, "Thank you."

I offer her a comforting smile. "They're sending you home, y'know."

Her pallid expression, always so sad and meek, breaks with a ray of hope that makes my own heart full. If I can't be reunited with my family, I'm glad that she will be at least.

I step into the car with my driver, the brunette and the other three in the second car. I get a quick flash of the brunette's face, a relieved smile stretching across it, the stress of her living nightmare finally receding to the calm of the just and the innocent and the delivered.

I did it, I tell myself. *We made it. I may just have a future to look forward to after all.* My car pulls away from the curb and my body is flushed with relief.

It doesn't last.

The explosion behind us is so close that I can feel the wave of heat pushing the car from behind. The flash of light fills the rearview mirrors, and I don't have to turn around in order to confirm what I already know.

The second car sits at the curb, chunks of metal still falling down around it, flames leaping up from within and beneath.

Even in the heat and the flames, a cold stone sinks in my gut as my KGB driver pulls me further and further from the burning wreckage and charred corpses within.

When the familiar guards bring me before Sobchak and

Dragunov again, I don't know if it is as a failure or as the lone success. The question would come down to who put the bomb in that second car.

When Sobchak says, "Congratulations, Agent Zolotov," I have my answer.

The KGB blew up the four failed candidates and always intended to, I realize. Of course, they couldn't just return them to their families, not knowing as much as they did and having seen as much as they have seen.

But what happened to the other two so-called diplomats? I hope my friend Ivanna is okay, suspecting that she may also have succeeded and is being assigned to a different case.

I realize that it is not my place to ask, and that stepping out of place could cost me everything. So I resolve myself to not knowing what happened to them until fate reveals it or until I can discover it for myself safely.

Until then there is information I need more urgently than that of my friend's fate; that of my own.

Sobchak drops a large folder on the desk. "Your first assignment."

I pick up the file and start looking through it; a dossier on a man whose handsome face is instantly familiar from my visions, his blond hair tinged with gray streaks, a roguish smile and white teeth. I am careful not to react although my heart skips a beat. *I can't believe this is the man of my dreams.*

"Senator Jonathan Caine," Dragunov says, "Washington DC. He is said to be a rising star in the senate, with personal access to President Kennedy. His interests seem to lay in helping the poor and eradicating organized crime."

My eyes scan the pages, my mind racing with second-guesses. *Am I to kill this man? Seduce him? Blackmail or otherwise destroy him?* Perhaps all three?

Sobchak says, "Get close to him, win his trust. Find out everything he knows and thinks and desires. We need to know what he will do before he does it; what those around him will do before they do it. You understand?"

I nod my head. "Yes, KomDiv Sobchak. But, and I mean no disrespect, aren't there other senators who would be more suitable subjects for this mission, perhaps one who sits on the Senate Foreign Relations Committee, or -- ?"

"Send a Russian spy into the offices of the Senator most intimately associated with our own government? We want information from them, not the other way around. And nobody with a specialty in this cold war of ours would be fooled. It is more important that we have eyes and ears in the senate, and best if we can control one or more of the senators, eventually secure their representation of our best interests."

"I see, of course."

"I will be following your progress closely," Agent Dragunov says, more than a suggestion of the lurid in his tone.

"Do well and there will be other assignments," Sobchak says. "Do poorly, and there will not be."

The threat to my life can hardly have been more clearly expressed, but at this point it isn't new information. I'll spend the rest of my life expecting death at any and every turn, for me or for someone near me, a lover or an enemy or both.

Fear of death; that is my life now.

CHAPTER FIVE

"I'm not afraid of death. It's the stake one puts up in order to play the game of life." -- Jean Giraudoux

January 1963

We fly into the United States on a commercial airline, having to make several stops so that our arrival cannot be traced directly to the Kremlin or the KGB. Agent Dragunov accompanies me, and I discover he'll be shadowing me almost at all times. He'll have other duties, but I will be high on his list of priorities. My success or failure will never be far from the eyes and ears of the beast himself, KomDiv Sobchak, and of course of the beast's handlers as well.

Everybody must serve somebody, after all.

Dragunov's American accent is quite good, as is mine. I have chosen to model my own on the flatter, Midwestern tones and phrasings. Dragunov has chosen a New England accent, with broader vowels and a distinctive cadence.

"We have secured you a position as Senator Caine's personal assistant," he says, handing me another dossier, this one thick with glossy black-and-white photographs. The first is of Caine himself, the same picture that was included in his own personal dossier.

"These people are his staff," Dragunov says. The first picture under Caine's is of a less-handsome man, his unsmiling face a terse and bitter mask. His dark brown hair is thinning, wire-frame glasses over his angular face.

"Chief of Staff/Administrative Assistant Daniel Oglvy, fifty-six years old; reports directly to Caine. He runs the rest of the staff, the senator's offices, evaluates the possible political outcome of various legislative proposals and constituent requests. Caine relies on him, and he'll be suspicious of you. Try to work around him if you can. If you can't, try harder."

The next photo presents the face of an older woman, her wrinkled skin, sagging jowls and excessive makeup suggesting her age at nearer to sixty than fifty.

"Vivian Galbraith," Dragunov says, "Caine's legislative director. She manages the legislative assistants and tends to the chief legislative priorities of the senator."

"So, the Chief of Staff handles what other people want from the senator, but the legislative director handles what the senator wants from other people."

"Quite so," Dragunov says, nodding. "I know that our tests are stringent, but surely you can see as well as I that they produce the best candidates."

I try not to smile. "I had excellent teachers," I say, hoping he doesn't see through the excessive flattery of my insincerity.

"You still have much to learn," Dragunov says as I flip to the next photo and profile. "Legislative assistant Myron St. Matthews," Dragunov says of the handsome, smiling young man trying to charm me from the black-and-white photo.

Dragunov adds, "He's primarily a strategist. The senator has a legislative cause, he gives it to his legislative director -- "

"And she turns it over this fellow. He seems... enthusiastic."

"Like most Americans, overly so. He's well-known as a social climber, an aggressive and opportunistic sort. Some speculate that he used telephone wiretaps to blackmail others competing for his position. This man's love isn't politics, or even his career, but success; in any field, at any price. He happened to choose an excellent field for a man of his perspective."

I look at that smiling face, eyes just a little too close together. But a closer look at the smile reveals the frown beneath it, that optimist's expression failing to obscure the soulless empty blackness that echoes behind it, endless and empty and lifeless like the Universe itself.

Another picture, another white man, this one about the same age as the grinning greed-head St. Matthews. But unlike the other man, this one is pudgy, with thick eyeglasses and shaggy black hair.

"Legislative correspondent Nathan Fellowsby," Dragunov says. "Research, letter writer, spends almost of his career in a library or back room typing. Get close to him if you can. A woman like you should have no problem turning him to your purposes, whatever they might be on a given day. You will need help, Aleksandra, and I won't be there to provide it."

"Then why will you be there?"

"To make sure you don't need too much of it. To see that you are faithfully serving the State. To kill you before you can defect."

The words ring in the back of my mind. Again, not new information, but hearing it brings more gravity to the information, a refreshed sense of urgency. And the cold fact that I am so helpless to defend myself that Dragunov would tell me so bluntly what might have otherwise have been kept secret feels like the chill of the grave itself.

Another photo reveals a woman, my system registering a slight relief to see that I will not be entirely surrounded by male energy. And even though I know that female energy can be its own obstacle, I've always made friends with girls, and I know this is a skill that will serve me well and may even save my life.

"Deloris Brooks," Dragunov says, "press secretary. Can you imagine such a thing?"

"A secretary to deal with the press?"

"A press that dares to deal directly with a high-ranking politician. When the American empire crumbles, this will be why. Americans think they have a right to know everything their government knows. They don't, of course, but given that illusion, they seem to be placated. Miss Brooks helps to maintain that delusion."

I say, "Miss? She can't be under thirty. But she's not married?" Off Dragunov's suspicious look, I say, "If she is interested in men, she may already have the senator's attention. And if not, that's something I want to know."

"So you can use it to secure her as an ally. Very good,

Aleksandra, very good."

There are two other photos and single-page profiles. Dragunov glances at them and shrugs. "Not important. The black man is Senator Caine's driver," he says of Tige, whose stoic face and chauffeur's cap suggest his function. "The boy is just an intern." I take a look at young Ralphie Adler's face, a proud and excited smile between his smooth, whisker-free cheeks.

"Those men will be of little help to you," Dragunov says, "but you will be coming into contact with them, so take care not to reveal yourself in anyway, to them or anyone. Concentrate your efforts on the senator."

I nod, trying to imagine circumventing all these other people, each harried and hurried and hampered by their own duties and agendas. "What will I be doing for the senator as his personal assistant?"

"You'll do whatever the senator wants you to do, is that understood?" Dragunov's voice is a quick snap of authoritarian rule, suppressing my naiveté. "The senator is recently divorced."

"I am to be his concubine?"

"If that is what he wishes, absolutely. But you will bring him his breakfast, run his errands, pick up his pet doggie's filthy waste from the yard if that is what he wishes. Win his trust and eventually, he will open up to you. If this requires that you first open up to him, so to speak, then so be it."

Washington was cold, frigid with a hint of snow on the horizon. It reminded me of home, of Siberia where our spring would be like this. I loved this time of year. Dragunov escorts me to the apartment building where we both will have small, one-room dwellings, his one floor above mine. It is not much distance, but I'm relieved not to have him right next door.

To say my apartment is stark would a serious overstatement. Mother Russian didn't spare any expense on accommodations. The irony of the situation struck me. They want me to get classified secrets worth millions, but they couldn't even give me a place that was a little bit comfy. It was like the story my grandfather told me once about the way they used to motivate soldiers in World War II – retreat and we will shoot you. Looking around can be cause for depression.

I've just flown thousands of miles to live in an apartment that is barely furnished: the living room was outfitted with a large, burgundy clothe chair, hideous, pea green ottoman, rickety coffee table and a black and white television; the bedroom is not much better - plain wooden dresser and armoire set, plus a bed that has an obvious dip in the center noticeable even with the shabby quilt on top.

The cupboards and drawers in the kitchen are equally uninspiring: four plates, four cups, four bowls, eight forks, knives and spoons, and four drinking glasses. The cutlery is flimsy; the dishes cheap plastic. I think it is called Melmac; cut-rate and scratched from previous use. I didn't come from rich roots, but at least we had a home that was well furnished with old Russian furniture, china handed down through the generations, linens and cutlery that didn't bend when used. No, I didn't hail from wealth, but I did have a bed that didn't cause back pain rather than rest.

I stand alone now abandoned by Dragunov looking out the only window in the living room, the lights of the United States capital flickering and twinkling in the darkness; a thousand points of light, the black and white television blathering on about the news in Washington.

A neon sign advertising this dump flashes on and off, orange and annoying. At least I sleep in the other room where only the cacophony of belching cars, backfiring trucks and the occasional scream accompany my attempt at sleeping. I miss the silence and soft sounds of nature at home. I don't think I will ever hear those sweet, comforting sounds again.

***

My first day at Senator Caine's office is a whirlwind of activity. I don't even catch a glimpse of the senator all day. Instead, I spend most of my time being sent from one staff member to another. Without the Senator's actual presence in the office, his personal assistant is left to acclimate and prepare me for whatever need the senator might need next.

And since nobody ever seems to sit down, I spend a lot of time and energy following around one person after another. I'm first introduced to Legislative Director Vivian Galbraith, who puts her liver-spotted hand to her breast every time she mentions the senator by name, as though she were saluting his very being.

"The Senator loves ballroom dancing, and he's magnificent at it," she says, walking with surprising quickness for a woman of her age and stocky build. "He's dedicated to helping the poor people of this country, which is a pretty fancy dance all its own. But mind you, he's pretty great at *that* too. So my advice would be to toss some change to any bum you both pass, and you'll have to be pretty quick to beat him to the punch. And..."

"And...?"

After a brief pause, Vivian adds, "And brush up on your waltz and your flamenco." *Does my job include dancing with him? What a strange custom.* Amid the constant din of phones ringing, typewriter's clattering and people muttering, somebody calls out Vivian's name, and we both turn to see Myron St. Matthews holding up a telephone and pointing at it.

Vivian turns to me and says, "Follow me," and we cross the room toward Myron. As Vivian takes the phone from Myron, she says, "Ali something, the senator's new personal assistant."

"Aleksandra," I say, adding, "*Tomanek*, Aleksandra *Tomanek*, from Wisconsin." Pudgy comes to mind when I look at him; he reminds me of a snowman with glasses. Unlike most snowmen, Myron's countenance is sour, his lips frozen in a permanent downturn.

Contempt for me, huh? Narrowed eyes, he squints through his glasses. Even if he smiled, his balding, out-of-shape physique would not be attractive. I doubt he's been found attractive by anyone in quite a long time. I watch his gaze flit away from sizing me up to the young intern hurrying past with papers in his arms. Myron smiles, licking his lips. *So, you like little boys, do you?* I tuck that tidbit away for the future.

His attention and gaze return to me, looking me up and down. He sniffs. "Kinda small for a plains girl. But I'm sure you'll do. Just keep one thing in mind."

There is silence between us. "And that is?"

"Stay the hell out of my way. I've been here for eight

months, and full terms with two senators before Caine. No way I'm letting some cheese-farming, floozy muscle in on my action. You can personally assist him all you want, but if you wind up on my bad side, I'll take you out."

Is this supposed to scare me? This eblan is threatening me? Govno, do you have any idea who you're talking to? I could kill you without breaking a sweat.

"Will do, Mr. St. Matthews. I'll make a point of staying out of your way." I valiantly try to keep the sarcasm out of my voice. *You hui, cocksucker, if I have the chance, I will see you gone from my sphere of influence. You won't last to serve a fourth senator if I have my way*. I nod, my lips turning up into a stiff smile.

"I don't recall Vivian introducing me," Myron squints his eyes, "just you."

Govno! I keep my face neutral. *Quick think of something.* "Vivian told me about you on our way across the room. What a great woman."

"Yeah, she's real faithful to the senator; it will probably be her undoing in the end. Another little bit of advice; this is Washington, sweetie. Trust nobody, love nobody, look out for number one, and that's you."

Behind us, a man clears his throat. I turn to see another pudgy man who I recognize as Legislative Correspondent Nathan Fellowsby. His disposition is friendlier, and he's smiling through his chubby jowls under his thick glasses, Nathan nods politely at me as he hands St. Matthew several sheets of white paper covered in black type. Does every man in Washington eventually wind up chubby and wearing glasses?

"Here's the senator's speech on that waste bill; thought you'd like to have a look."

"Of course I do, Fellowsby. When have I not?"

"Well, that's why I thought it."

"Any word on that business, on... the island?"

"The... oh, you mean Cuba?"

Myron frowns at Nathan and juts his head to indicate I am standing within earshot, a supposedly secretive motion that failed to slither around me notice.

Nathan just shakes his head. He turns to me and extends his hand. "Nathan Fellowsby, legislative correspondent."

"Aleksandra *Tomanek*, the senator's personal assistant."

"Welcome aboard, Aleksandra. Say, that's quite a pretty name. German?"

"Oh no, heavens no," I say with a nervous giggle. "Polish, actually."

"*Tomanek* is Polish?" His smile gives way to a bit of confusion.

"Shortened a couple of generations ago from something too long to pronounce.

"Nice, your people make tremendous sausages. Glad to have you aboard. Come on, I'll introduce you around." *Sausages? What is he talking about? Well, at least he's friendlier*. I make a note to look up the sausage reference.

I follow him as we step away from Myron St. Matthews. I turn to give him a smile and tell him it was nice to meet him, but he's already reading Nathan's speech for the senator and doesn't care enough about me to see me off with the slightest courtesy. *Americans are all rude and fat.*

Nathan leads me to Deloris Brooks, whose fading beauty only accentuates her underlying sorrow. She smiles at me, but I know she's faking it. She looks me up and down, the differences between my own body and hers fairly natural for a fifteen-year gap. It isn't my fault that I was born more recently than she, even if I instantly have the impression that she is ready to hold me personally accountable.

Nathan introduces me and Deloris shakes my hand, baubles rolling on her bony wrist. I say, "I'm so happy to meet you."

Deloris just looks at me, not sure what to make of my comment, my appearance, my presence, my anything and my everything. I'm not sure if she wants to turn around and run or throttle me death with the desk lamp. I continue smiling not sure what of my next move.

She picks up the phone and starts dialing a number, saying, "If you're the senator's personal assistant, what are you doing here while he's in a meeting with Senators Geason, Bartlet and Donahue?"

I'm not sure, which is the only reasonable answer I can give. "They sent me here."

"Who did," Nathan asks, "the agency?"

Not exactly sure what she means and not wanting to give away anything, I say, "I just graduated from college. There was a program, to apply for this position."

Deloris asks, "As personal assistant to a United States senator without any real experience?"

Nervously, I say, "My daddy, he's friends with a man, I really shouldn't say who..."

"Forget it," Deloris says, raising the telephone receiver to her ear. "This is Washington, here everybody's daddy knows somebody, they really shouldn't say who..."

"Don't mind her," Nathan says to me, "she's always under a lot of stress."

Deloris says, "Take a good look, sweetie; I used to be pretty too. And it wasn't that long ago." Deloris turns her attention back to the phone and says into it, "Yeah, Deloris Brooks from Senator Jonathan Caine's office. I need to look over that transcript you're using on the waste management story..."

Nathan leads me away with the gentle jut of his jowly head. He says, "As long as the senator's not here, maybe you'd like to do me a little favor?"

"Well, um, of course, sure, as long as the senator doesn't need me."

Nathan shrugs. "That seems to be the case. But I've got a five-page report that needs to be looked at. I don't see our intern around, so how'd you feel about running down, grabbing a quick pastrami on rye, extra mustard?"

I consider it, seeing an opportunity that would solidify this man as my friend, my ally, a weapon in my arsenal. And if the ammo for that weapon included fatty meats and mustard, so much the easier for me.

"Sure," I say, just as Vivian walks by, putting a ten dollar bill in my hand.

"Chinese chicken salad," Vivian says.

Before I get to the door, I'm holding sixty-five dollars and trying to keep five lunch orders straight, all of them from different types of restaurants.

I stand in the elevator thinking, this can't be what the KGB has in mind, unless they want me to poison the entire staff.

The day drags on and finally chubby, friendly Nathan walks me to my apartment building nearby. I convince him not to follow up to my room, letting him think he might find his way up there someday.

And I'm glad, because Dragunov's presence in my room is neither a shock nor welcomed.

"How was your first day on the job?"

I shrug, not giving him the satisfaction of having surprised me. "Didn't even lay eyes on the senator. I think I'm the personal assistant to everybody *but* the senator."

"See to it that it doesn't last," he says. "We didn't go to all this trouble and expense so you could deliver sandwiches to a bunch of fools and flunkies."

"Deliver... are you spying on me?"

"Of course," he says. "*That's* why I'm here."

"Well, I'm sorry to have wasted your time."

"Don't do it again."

"What am I supposed to do?" I ask, plopping down on the couch. "I'm the lowest rung on the ladder, I just got here and already half the people hate me just *because* I'm there. I can't start making demands. Now you and your caveman master are just going to have to be patient and back off or you'll blow the whole thing, and I'll be the one who has to pay for it."

Not showing any offense to my outburst, he says simply, "That's right, Aleksandra, you will."

The next day I spend the first few hours continuing to do errands for the rest of the senator's staff. I haul reams of blank paper, clear waste paper baskets, bring up food and even bags of soda pop to refill the office's refrigerator.

I also meet Ralphie Adler, the boyish and enthusiastic intern, who seems even more feminine than me. He gestures grandly, reacts broadly with a looping voice and bright, bulging eyes. "So *you're* the new P.A. I *heard* he was getting one. I *love* your hair; you are *so* pretty! I just *know* we're gonna be *best* friends!"

Ralphie is at one end of the spectrum, closest to my own lowly position. And at the other end, the only other member of the staff (besides the senator himself) I haven't met.

And my first contact with him is not an introduction.

Chief of Staff and Administrative Assistant Dan Oglvy sees me from across the room. I feel his eyes locking on me as an unfamiliar face, always unwelcome in political circles.

But instead of approaching me, he simply holds out his pointed finger, his voice loud and his words slow and definitive. "Who... is... that... young... woman?"

The entire office goes quiet, only the scattered ringing of the telephones underlying the new tension in the room. He's tall, with the bearing and command of a high-ranking officer.

Myron St. Matthews approaches him and whispers something into his ear. Then Dan glares at me from his position across the room, bellowing, "Personal assistant, is that what they're calling them now?"

He strides toward me, everyone in the office watching his

approach. Everything has ground to a halt and refuses to move until something happens between us.

And they don't have to wait long.

He arrives in front of me. "How old are you?"

"Nineteen."

He looks me over, sneering and snarling, his ice-cold eyes nearly freezing the blood in my veins. "Just stay the hell out of my way." This really is beginning to sound like a theme in this office.

Myron let out a surprised chuckle. "Ha! That's what I said."

"Shut up, brown-nose," Dan says without taking his eyes off me, even though I take it as more of an offensive gesture toward Myron than a lustful advance upon me. I get the feeling this man is into another type of woman altogether.

And I make a note of it.

"Yes sir," Myron says to Dan, backing away.

"What's all this?"

We turn at the voice, unfamiliar to me alone. But I know the face. Senator Jonathan Caine himself strides into the bullpen, that central area where most of the staff have their desks. He looks much like his picture, but even more handsome. The black-and-white of the photo did little to get across his healthy complexion, the whiteness of his teeth, the sparkle of his blue eyes, the graying hair that is more blonde than brown.

He smiles at me, extending his open hand. "Jon Caine," he says.

I take his hand, large and steady around mine. "Aleksandra *Tomanek*."

"Aleksandra?" the senator repeats. "That's a mouthful. You're my personal assistant, Alexsa.. Lexy?"

"Yes, Senator, I'm happy to be of any help I can be."

He shrugs, shaking his head. "This is Washington, Lexy, we all need as much help as we can get." He turns to Vivian. "You know what I need done, right?"

Vivian nods, her hand over her chest. "Absolutely, Senator Caine."

He turns back to me and smiles. "Welcome aboard." With that, he turns and strides down the hall, most of his staff following on his heels.

Vivian approaches me and puts her hand on my arm. "Let's go find a pen."

We spend a good amount of time outlining the personal tasks the senator will need me to do for him. And although I can't say I look forward to much of it, I feel that it's a big step toward completing the mission and a big step away from being the office slave which I was fast becoming.

***

Another lonesome night in Washington DC. After explaining to Dragunov that I'm getting access to the senator's personal living space, his dietary habits, a complete personal profile, I'm left to another night of staring at the flickering specks of light in that inky sea that flooded my apartment's only window.

I grew up in a small town in the Omsk, where there was little enough in the way of excitement. As a little girl, I'd dreamed of adventure and heroics, of grandeur and danger, of princes and heroes and journeys to far-off lands.

Now, here I am, a grown woman in the capital city of the one of the most powerful countries on Earth, working alongside one of the most powerful men in that city. I am strong and adult, capable enough to be sent on a mission of international intrigue and import.

Yet I'm confined to my room like a child, punished for a wrong-doing that was never my own, trapped in a world I not only never made but never really wanted. *There are no heroes here,* I realize, *only villains. No adventure, only danger. No romance or glory, only dishonesty, risk and fear and probably death at the end of it all.*

Still, the lights are so pretty, so bright, so small and yet so strong, cutting through the darkness that oppresses them and tries to smother their tiny glory. But they are not bowed, they shine on.

They survive.

And if they can, so can I.

***

The next day I am at the senator's buzzing office for a brief while in the morning, only to be told amid the confusion and hustle that I'm not supposed to be there at all. I am supposed to be executing the laundry list of chores to take care of on Senator Jon Caine's behalf. And I use the term *laundry list* without very much irony, as laundry is in fact very high on that list, but not before shopping for his groceries, sorting his mail and finding suitable gifts for the nieces of his ex-wife. I don't know much about what happened in that marriage, but if this man still wants to give gifts to the woman's nieces, I can only assume that he is a man of excellent character and strong emotional bonds.

I make a note of that valuable information, and any other insights I can glean from an otherwise tedious day of picking things up and dropping them off.

On the street, between one thing and another, things really start to pile up, and I'm not being figurative. My arms are spilling over with ten dress suits, each including two pair of pants and covered with a long plastic bag. It's not that they're heavy, which they are, but they keep sliding away from each other and falling to my feet.

Eventually, they all go cascading to the sidewalk, gathering around me like Joan of Arc's kindling.

I bend down and start scooping up the suits, turning with a start to hear, "Lemme help you out." I recognize him immediately, even though we haven't met. Tall, broad, dark-chocolate skin shimmering, his black chauffeur's uniform absorbing all light.

Tige Abrahmson, Senator Caine's driver, bends to help me collect the suits.

"Thank you so much, Tige."

He says, "You know me, too?"

"Too?"

He nods. "You're the senator's new girl."

I look him over, allowing the offense to take my expression. "I beg your pardon? I'm the senator's personal assistant; I'm not anybody's *girl*."

He considers me as he gathers the last of the suits, his expression stoic, grim. "My apologies. No offense intended. Just a saying."

I give it some thought. If I weren't the KGB's girl, I would have been even more offended, but it occurs to me that this man would make a powerful ally under the right circumstances. More often than not, men of power seek the advice of the least among their circle; drivers, shoe-shines, housekeepers.

I smile. "No offense taken. I'm Aleksandra."

"Tige. Can I give you a lift?"

I look at the limo, windows blacked out. "Don't you have to take the senator somewhere?"

"On my way to get her washed, actually. C'mon."

He walks over and pops open the trunk, setting the suits in his arms and mine flat in the trunk and closing the lid.

He opens the back door to the limo, but I insist on riding up front with him, as his equal and not his superior. At first he hesitates, as if being seen with a white woman in the front seat of a car could get him lynched; because in some parts of this country, it would.

But not here, in the country's capital, and the windows are tinted.

We glide past the crowded sidewalks, movers and shakes all pushing and shoving not only to get ahead, but simply to get by.

Tige says, "I've seen you around the office, Aleksandra. In fact, we were all shown pictures of you before you arrived... security measure, you understand." The Kremlin has done a thorough job, but I am still a little nervous to hear Tige take this line of conversation. "But how do you know me?"

I have to think fast. "Deloris mentioned you, she described you to a tee. Plus, the uniform and all, I guess I took a leap of faith."

Tige grunted, peering out the side window. "Anybody comes to this town does." We share a chuckle as Tige pushes the limo into a muscular left turn toward the senator's townhouse.

Tige leaves the limo double-parked as he helps me with the suits. After hanging them in the closet, Tige asks if there's somewhere else he can drop me before he has the limo washed and returns to the offices. I shake my head and allow him to go on with his way, content to walk to the drug store to pick up the senator's personal toiletries.

Ah, the glamor of Washington!

***

Another exchange with Dragunov separates my strenuous day from my monotonous night. It's easy enough to goad Dragunov into thinking I'm making strides in the mission to get close to Senator Caine. It's not much more progress than the day before; but we both know the mission will take some time, and that the progress I am making is enough to warrant a bit of leeway in my governance.

Before he leaves, I ask, "Where are you going tonight, Dmitry?" using the Americanized name he chose as his cover.

"Out," is his only answer, before stepping into the building hallway and slamming the door behind him. I think about his disposition. He'd shown an interest in me before, back in Moscow, but the threat of Sobchak's wrath kept him away. I even expressed an interest myself, hoping my positive enforcement of a possibly negative condition would further him toward doing what I wanted him to do.

It's one of the things I learned from Sobchak himself.

But here and now, there's nothing to keep him from pursuing me; and as far as he'd know, every reason and justification for doing so. Yet he doesn't.

And I'm not disappointed at all, of course. The last thing I need is for my own watchdog to be nipping at my heels. But the fact that he doesn't gives me pause, makes me wonder what other forces are acting upon him, constricting him.

Watching him.

Watching him as he watches me.

I know I'm surrounded on all sides. I remember the fiery explosion that took the lives of those four female KGB hopefuls. When Myron told me not to trust anybody in Washington, I didn't know then but I come to realize more and more that this includes anybody in Washington, no matter what country they're from. There are people around me I can't trust and that includes taxi drivers, beat cops, bums on the street. Anybody with eyes and ears and a heartbeat could be an enemy, sent by my own keepers to monitor my every move.

To kill me without a moment's notice if that is what the orders are.

And if so, I have no protection and no escape.

I stare out into that night, night after night after night, the grind of the days filled with pettiness and greed and ambition and even sloth giving way to nights of ceaseless worry and wonder and waiting.

Something has to give.

One night, after tending to a day's worth of the senator's dry cleaning and grocery shopping, I decide if I must die without warning, I want to see some of Washington DC's nightlife before I go.

After my routine meeting with the increasingly agitated Dragunov, I slip down the staircase to the rear exit of the apartment building lobby, a floppy hat pulled over my head, and step into the sultry heat of the Washington summer.

I stroll through the city at night, the bustle and energy not diminished by the dark of night. If anything, darkness seems to bring out the true nature of the city. I find myself walking past the famous memorial dedicated to the United States president Abraham Lincoln. He sits on his great stone throne, a face nearly ferocious with determination, eyes glaring into a future that he would sacrifice himself to ensure. He faces eternal enemies, and faces them eternally. I look into those stone eyes of that great white giant and wonder what demons he faced within as much as without. And the whole world knows the price he paid and the prize he won.

I wonder what prize I'll win. I already have a pretty good vision of what price I'll pay.

Soon enough I find a nightclub, a line of young people waiting to get into a place whose blinking neon sign proclaims it, *DCGB's.*

I look over the line; mostly men, a lot of them with women in tow. No single women. So I step up to the beefy doorman in front of the entrance. I take off my hat and toss it away, shaking my blonde hair lose around my shoulders. I'm ready to say, *Senator Caine,* knowing the power his name carries in town. But I don't have to say a thing. My face does the asking; my body does the talking.

It's all part of the mission, I tell myself.

Once inside, I'm surrounded by flashing lights and loud music, a crowd so dense I would almost think they'd been imprisoned here but for their swaying hips, tight dresses, stylish hairstyles, everybody smiling and dancing.

If this is an American gulag, I tell myself, it might just be time to turn myself in.

"Martini," somebody says behind me. I turn to see a

handsome young man, his black hair short and clean, even his black suit seeming to hang relaxed on his young and powerful frame.

"Pardon me?"

He repeats, "Martini," then adds, "what do you say?"

I look around, suddenly feeling like the only person in the room without a drink. Knowing it will never compete in potency with the vodka of my own home town, I nod and shrug and smile and offer up a few more unnecessary indications of my acceptance.

Reading my awkwardness, he says, "I'll take that as a yes." He turns to the bar, gesturing with the bartender, who nods his understanding.

I let him buy me the drink and I enjoy it, even having to tolerate his stammering seduction.

"In this town, it's all about who you know. And now, you know me."

I smile, sipping my martini, cold yet warming, sweet and sour. "And who do you know?"

"Senator Hanson, from Missouri. Great guy, great boss."

"You're his personal assistant?"

"Personal -- ?   No, I'm an intern for his legislative coordinator. Still, he's a heck of a nice guy. Gonna have a great future in this town, probably make it to the big game someday."

"The big game?"

"The Mighty Whitey! The top job."

"President, you think he's going be president someday?"

He shrugs and smiles in a way that I know he thinks is sexy, and probably is when he's not drunk, and when his intended hasn't been to the places I've been to. He says, "It's a dirty job but, hey, somebody's gotta screw it up, right?"

He laughs. After a moment or two, I decide to laugh with him.

What's the harm? I figure. I think the same thing when another man, not quite as young, offers to buy me my next drink. Three drinks later, I'm quite used to my new perspective. I'm not quite as used to the walk home, however.

I don't arrive until after midnight, but I creep in quietly and thankfully I don't have to contend with Dragunov and his growing dissatisfaction. *Does he want to rape me?* I wonder, *kill me, marry me? All three?*

What's the difference? I have to ask myself. If I don't get close to Senator Caine soon, I'll be dead anyway. But I'm not dead yet.

I pass out for the first time since the train ride into Moscow, when I shared the company of fourteen other young, unwilling volunteers, all of whom are dead now, for all I know.

The next morning, I wake up wondering if I hadn't joined them. I've had liquor before, of course, but not so much so fast. And when I did it was vodka only, not a prolonged mixture of every type of booze a man could buy a woman he wants to bed.

I push through the headache and the dry mouth and the burning, reddened eyes to take care of the senator's fish tank, which needs cleaning, and the fireplace of his Jamestown townhouse, which also needs cleaning; each by a true professional.

Then there is the dry cleaning, another armful of suits and a dozen dress shirts. *How many suits does one man need?* I'm glad not to have greater responsibilities, given my lessened physical state, even gladder that I have several hours before having to appear before Dragunov for our daily review.

By the time I see him, I've recuperated enough to feign being tired only, and I *am* tired. The truth always makes lying easier. And I begin to notice more and more about Dragunov;

his fearful twitch when I mention the beast, his master KomDiv Sobchak.

During a lull in our discussion, perhaps because of my weakened state and perhaps because of my progressed confidence, I finally ask, "What is it with you and the beast? I know you hate him, and fear him."

He glares at me, and for the first time I wonder how sober he is. His head sways on his shoulders as he looks around my dim and small living room. He almost speaks, but stops himself.

I let silence coax him to say what he's been waiting years to say.

"You have parents," he finally says. "Maybe kids, too, I dunno..." I shake my head. "Well, imagine what your parents would say, what your father would say, if his boss wanted to sleep with you."

I think about it, able to retrieve memories of the lustful glances I'd attracted from my father's associates, my brother's friends, my own classmates and teachers.

Then Dragunov adds, "Now imagine that you're a boy."

I remember my visions of the beast Sobchak intermingled with images of naked boys; tortured, crying and dying.

Dragonuv was one of those boys?

No wonder he's so sad, I think to myself. And so afraid.

We're all afraid.

But fear drives the people in Washington, I begin to realize; fear and greed and love and hate and everything in between. For sure, they're driven by *something.*

I am driven by sheer momentum, by the force of everyone around me. Certainly, my first few weeks are not driven by my own initial progress. Even as I feel I can justify a rocky start, as the days go on, my sense of accomplishment and my ability to exude it are eroded by a creeping sense of futility and fatalism.

I'm never going to get close to Senator Caine by being the one who organizes his aquarium maintenance and serve as his dry cleaning delivery service. And if I fail to get close to Caine and to extract some worthy data, I know I won't get a second chance; not at Caine, or at another mission.

Or at life.

And Dragunov's steadily increasing ire at my recurring inebriation doesn't make things any easier. Fortunately, his own steadily increasing inebriation helps me deflect his ire even as it inflates.

Drunkenness is the enemy of reason, and without reason our mission cannot succeed. Unfortunately, both of us are tending to indulge ourselves in this manner. I know why I'm doing it; boredom, restlessness mixed with moments of terror. And I know why Dragunov does it; the original serpents from the legend of Hercules' infancy; the venomous and lethal doubt and pride.

Between the two of us, Sobchak is likely to dispatch men to withdraw us both from this failed enterprise. I know more than ever that such men are probably not far off; reporting every drink, every laugh, every smile.

But those things do come more easily here, more readily. In the United States, everybody seems to be smiling, everyone is either truly happy or feels the need to exude a facade of happiness. In Siberia, quiet misery is much more the height of fashion.

But I never was all that miserable in my childhood. My loving parents saw tot that. I spent hours in the fields of the Omsk and spinning tales in my own imagination and listening to Papa tell me stories of far off places. If Omsk was bleak and miserable, I never knew it. It wasn't until I was taken did I know bleak loneliness and fear. Now, in the United States, given the chance to drink from the font of life, I am not about to deny myself.

As for Dragunov, I can only assume that denial has already crushed him, and that his only option is to burrow deeper into that mountain in hopes of somehow emerging from the other end, and not merely to dig his own grave.

Whether those two would not amount to the same thing in the end, I cannot say any more than I can predict my own precarious future. There may be spies all around me; every human outreach I make may bring me an inch closer to the lid of my coffin being pulled down over me. I go out at night to attempt to grasp a tiny touch of life. *I want to go home.*

In hopes of obtaining that which I long for, I risk losing it all.

My life is not my own, I know that. Who am I kidding? I have always known it. It belongs to the State. I belong to Mother Russia. And if this life is not mine to lose, if they will take it at any moment for any reason, then let them. I will take what I can and leave the rest.

So I revel, I indulge. I sway my hips and raise my hands, using my woman's body the way most Western women use theirs; as a beacon, a flashing light in the expansive, permanent midnight of Western bacchanalia.

The men are a swarm around me, buzzing and touching and even biting a little bit. I never felt unattractive, and I know the power I have over men, even if most reasonably attractive women hold the same sway.

But I'm not like most women. The KGB made certain of that.

In one club, the endless thunder and clang of the Rock 'n' Roll gave way to a slower, somber tune, the twang of a steel guitar behind the saddened voice of a lonely woman.

"You like Patsy Cline?" I turn to see a handsome young man standing next to me. Not sure how to answer, I wait for him to add, "*I Fall To Pieces,* by Patsy Cline. They never play it unless you ask for it as a special request."

I hear her sing the refrain and I nod, understanding.

"And you requested it?"

He nods, knowing that I also understand.

So I share a dance with him, his body tall and lean in front of me, swaying to the folksy rhythm. He even spins me once, a move I find quite exhilarating and even romantic.

Soon the rock music returns, drums banging and lead guitars playing those rapid-fire licks, the horns and the black girls singing to the postman, to their unfaithful lovers.

But still, poor Patsy's lovely lament rings in my ears even as the stress and the strain of the nightlife wears me down, little by little and the pressure and pain of my recent, turbulent change of life weighs on me heavier and heavier.

As the days become weeks, my strength begins to ebb. Hours of work push me to my limit, and hours of drinking and dancing and lights and music only extend the reach of that limit. My head begins to constantly ache, my ears to ring; my fingers grow numb and nearly useless.

I come to forget the feeling of being in total control, the strength that comes with a healthy body and an unpolluted mind. But what purpose are these things being put to? The health of my body is only a tool of the State, my mind a weapon to be used and then discarded when no longer functioning at full capacity or replaced by a sleeker, more effective model. If I am to lose these things anyway, I'd rather put them to some pleasurable use and not volunteer them entirely to the pleasure of my government and those who abuse her, and me, to their own ends.

But this comes at a price, one I feel that I'm paying little by little instead of in one hideous lump sum.

I can't seem to stop myself. There's so much excitement and glamor and sheer humanity in these Washington nights, I can't sit idly by and not be a part of it. *I'll have the rest of eternity for that.*

Each night I push myself further; the music seems louder, the drinks stronger, the men pushier, the women sexier. As we've heard about the United States, the people's clarion call seems to be *more more more!*

And they're getting it, every day and in every way. *Surely,* I think to myself, *this decadence cannot last, not for me or for these others.* Nobody can live long or happily with this kind of routine.

I am determined to give it my all, and I do my best, wearing my tight red dress cradling the curves of my hips and waist, my round, firm breasts just as high and proud as any American woman's. I shake my long, blonde hair, letting it mesmerize and astound as it falls over my face; lips pouting, eyes dipped closed as I drink in the driving rhythms.

After too many hours to count, I know I have to go back to my apartment. I accept an offer from the nearest man to drive me home, then politely refuse his advances in front of the building two blocks north of my own. I don't want anybody knowing where I live, or having anybody who does know where I live see me being dropped off by some strange American at three o'clock in the morning.

I let him drive off and then turn for the short walk home.

The street starts to bend and twist in front of me, double-vision making it hard to concentrate on where I am going. The ringing in my ears throws me off balance, my legs uncertain and my body oddly asymmetrical. My stomach turns, nauseous, the street looms in front of me as I bob and weave and barely manage to stay on my feet and take that next reckless step toward my apartment.

I almost make it, when a small car skids to a halt in front of me, nearly running me over. Or perhaps it is more correct to say that I almost fall under the car.

The end result would be the same. And a familiar voice slides out of the car. "Lexy?"

I turn, swaying and squinting to focus on none other than Senator Jonathan Caine. *Oh no, I don't want him to see me in this state.* "Senator Caine, I..."

"Get in," he says, head tilting toward the passenger door of his car. I step around, weaving a bit and unable to stop, before climbing in. The car is warm and dark, and filled with the scent of his cologne. "Looks like you had quite a night."

I look myself over, flushed with embarrassment as he drives forward. "I had some... interesting experiences, met some people. Nobody of consequence."

"Knowing this town, nobody of any truth, either." He adds, "You really shouldn't be alone on the streets at this time of night. Where's your place?"

"It's actually... we just drove past it." He shoots me a confused look. Without making him ask, I explain, "I thought it'd be more... less conspicuous if I ..."

Senator Caine chuckles, "The old two-blocks-down routine. Classic. You're a smart girl, Lexy, and just a little bit devious. You'll do well in Washington."

"Senator, I --"

"Please, Lexy... Jon."

I can't help but smile as Jon takes us around the block. I say, "Jon, I want you to know that, even though I was out, I, um, I won't let it affect my work."

Jon says, "You've been doing all right so far, but it's bound to catch up with you, Lexy."

I try to think of something clever to say, but I can't. It takes most of my energy to stay upright and hold back the punchbowl's worth of different liquors sloshing around inside me.

"Which building?" Jon asks, the car slowing down around

us as he pulls up to the curb. I point and he stops, double-parking and shutting off the engine. "You better let me see you up."

I struggle to stand up again, nearly falling on my face. "No, that's all right. I can manage on my own." *Great, these heels will be the death of me.*

"I will see you to your apartment, Lexy." His tone brooks no argument, and I really don't have the strength to do it, anyway. *You are the man of my dreams, and the first time we meet outside of work, I'm drunk. What a great first impression.*

"I'm fine." I start anyway, and he holds up his hand, his normally pleasant disposition and countenance darkening.

"I won't have you stumbling and staggering towards your apartment in the middle of the night unescorted. How many times have you done this since you got here from the Midwest?"

Embarrassment. Can I say many, many, many times? I remain silent not meeting his gaze.

"That many, huh?" I think he's angry with me. Well, that's new.

"I don't need your help," I insist making a grab for my purse and missing. I don't need this man judging me. I can drink myself senseless, if I want. As long as I turn up for work tomorrow, who is he?

Jon sighs and holds me steady as he closes the door to his car. I point. "Let's go. Which way?" He starts to escort me into my building.

"Didn't you hear me, Jon," my words are slurred.

"Yes." He keeps walking towards the building. His arm is around my waist, so it's impossible for me to stand still. I am forced to walk with him. My head is spinning, and I allow myself to lean on him as we walk up the stairs to my second-floor apartment. Things get blurry fast. My imbalance from the street only feels more advanced, my muscular control even less so. The more I lean on Jon, the more I want to lean on him and the more I feel that I need to lean on him. I also don't want to vomit which would be the cherry on top of my evening.

My apartment is dark. Jon is practically carrying me now, my feet dragging and my head hanging as he slides the straps of my red dress from my shoulders and lets it fall to a crumpled red mass at my feet. He stops at my door, rifling through my purse with one hand, holding me steady with the other until he finds my keys. He opens the door, and drags me across the threshold turning on the lights. I can't believe he ignored my protestations.

ROBERT FURST & ALAN PARKER

"I've come home drunk many a night, and I didn't need a man to escort me anywhere." My words feel like I'm talking with cotton balls in my mouth.

"Are you listening to me?"

"Yes," I hear water running in the kitchen. I'm sitting on my sofa. He returns with a large glass of water and two pills. "Take these and drink all of the water."

"No, I don't want to." I try to push his hand away, but he persists.

"If you don't drink all of this water and take these pills, I'm going to spank you, Lexy. Then you're going to take them and drink the water." *Wait, what did he say? Is he crazy?*

He offers me the glass of water again, and I weigh my options. *Do I want to risk getting him angrier? I have to keep this job in order to do the mission.* I start to drink, then puase, put the two pills in my mouth and look up at him bleary eyed.

"What did you say?"

"You heard me," he replies. "Now finish drinking so I can get you to bed." *To bed? He's putting me to bed?* I finally finish the glass of water, my head swimming and my stomach threatening to explode. I feel worse than if I wanted to barf. American liquor is so much different than vodka. I love it, but

I'm not sure it loves me.

He picks me up off the sofa and transfers me to the bed. He sighs and starts to take off my shoes. I am exhausted, drunk and very nearly unconscious. I can't keep my eyes open any longer, and I don't care anymore what he does. I hear him say that we will talk in the morning, as I close my eyes against my own counsel, and the world swims away into hazy nothingness.

***

The night sputters past in fits and starts, blocks of what feel like sleep interrupted by dreams, images, visions that seem too real. I see Dragunov standing by my bed, his voice a sinister whisper. "You *shalava*, you let him undress you and you were too drunk to seduce him?" I feel the bed shaking slightly, a heavy pressure on top of me.

I dream that I'm being crushed by something, imagining the faces of the miners who attacked me in that Omsk field years ago. I look up and it's as if it's really happening, yet it isn't.

Not Omsk, I tell myself in a dream state of half-clarity. *Not the miners. Not my brothers.*

Not Senator Jon Caine.

But somebody. shalava, Why are you calling me a dirty slut in Russian; you know we. must not use Russian ever on our mission. Are you drunk? You know that will get us exposed. Americans are paranoid about the Russians. One word and we could be found out, you idiot.

The dark room and a blurred man's face punctuate the undulating darkness of a nauseous and restless sleep. Smells surround me, subtle pressure and a steady rhythm preventing my body from recovering its strength, its energy.

I can feel him inside me, someone, my head tilting and shaking as I try to focus, vainly trying to push the name out of my mouth. *Jon? Dragunov? Sobchak?*

"Jon*?*" My saliva tastes vile.

"Nyet." I hear a whisper in my ear, and then my mouth is full. There's a salty taste, movement in an out and I gag but it continues. "Sosi moi hui sooka!" I remember the little boy and Sobchak. I am the little boy, and Sobchak must have found out about my failings. This is his punishment, and if I want to live I must take his cock like he says and like it. I let it continue until a lot of saltiness fills my mouth. I hear a groan . . . pleasure. I want to vomit, but can't. There's no place for the vomit to go, so the saltiness and slime slides down my throat. I gag and swallow it.

Another whisper, an admonition. "Remember your mission, *shalava*, or I will do this again."

"Yes, Comrade Sobchak." I hear a soft chuckle then silence and I am alone again.

Darkness. Unconsciousness pulls me back from the brink of clarity and control. The only thing resembling reason which remains in my drunken brain is that I admit to myself that Jon had been right.

It *has* caught up with me.

***

July 1963

The next morning, I wake up feeling like my body was tossed out the window, and my landing was on hard concrete. I feel lucky to be alive. My legs hurt, my crotch aches, my skin is clammy, the sheets are damp, my mouth tastes like a sewer. The air is musty, dewy with a human musk. *What a great way to start the morning.*

I think back to the night before, realizing at once that it hadn't been a dream. I can't recall exactly what I said, if anything, to whomever it was who had invited himself to use my body the night before.

Was it Sobchak? Was it Jon? My scrambled memory isn't helping and neither is the dull pounding headache. *Dragunov?* One of the KGB shadow agents I've so often imagined snooping around behind every corner? *The guy from the club who drove me home? Somebody else entirely?*

I can't think anymore. I push myself into the shower, legs slow to respond to my brain's weakened requests. My whole body wants simply to collapse and stay down for good.

I can't be weak. I have a job and a mission and the one is reliant upon the other. My life is at stake, which is incentive enough for a hot shower; not to mention the filth and degradation that I feel all around me, inside and out, that even a hundred showers won't wash away.

The water is hot against my skin; rejuvenating, pushing my blood through my veins with greater eagerness, restoring my vision and hearing to some semblance of functionality. I wash every crevice, letting the soapy film cling to my aching body. relishing the blanket of hot water wrapped around my back and legs and arms and breasts.

I dress and get to the office, only a minute or two late.

I'm not surprised to hear Jon call my name shortly after I arrive. Vivian gives me a sympathetic look, as if I am about to be sent to the gulag. Myron snickers, his smile only making the same grim assertion.

Jon stands up behind his desk and gestures with an open

hand to one of the two leather easy chairs facing him. I sit, the burgundy leather creaking beneath me.

"You look better this morning," he says. I know what he means, but given the strange occurrences in my room in the dead of the night, I feel it's best to let him continue, make himself clearer and maybe make the events of the evening clearer, too. He adds, "I'm glad to see you can still bounce back from such a night. Lexy, I really do want you to be more careful. Too much drinking and partying; not only is it bad for your health, but it can leave a young woman vulnerable to... all sorts of unpleasant circumstances."

I feel my blood run cold. My growing admiration and respect for Jon is chilled by the ugly realization that the man who took advantage of me last night may well be standing right in front of me now.

I didn't believe it before, because I didn't want to believe it. "You sound like you know what you're talking about. And no wonder."

He turns his head, squinting in confusion. "How do you mean?"

"You said it would catch up with me, and it sure did. Guess you decided if somebody was going to deliver my comeuppance, it may as well be you."

He shakes his head now, his confusion seeming to give way to slow realization just as his nurturing tone recedes in favor of the quick snap of anger and defensiveness. "Lexy, I don't know exactly what you're talking about, but I put you to bed and that's where I left you, completely untouched. If we had been in a relationship, well, I know you're young, but I wouldn't have just left you there."

"What does that mean?" I challenge. I'm angry at him.

"It means that you wouldn't be out in the middle of the night staggering home completely drunk. I wouldn't allow it." He was clearly angry, but so was I.

I always have to push the envelope of reason. "You wouldn't allow it!" I keep my voice steady. American men are arrogant; no, Jon Caine is an arrogant idiot. I get up to leave. I'm done with this conversation.

"Sit down." Jon's voice is as quiet as my own, but the tone is unmistakable. If I make a move towards the door, there will be consequences. I'm not sure what the consequences will be, but they will be something. I can't afford to lose this job.

I sit on this overstuffed chair, and it's a good thing that I am sitting, because my newly nervous knees feel like they would have buckled. Now the confusion is mine, and my own anger gives way to utter embarrassment and shame.

Jon asks me, "You didn't go back out after I left you to bring some strange man to bed?" He has brought his voice back under control.

"No, I, of course not..." Now my shame becomes horror.

Jon says, "You're saying somebody crept into your room and raped you last night?" His anger survives his new compassion, but I get the feeling the anger is more protective *of* me than directed *at* me. What was with this man? He plays rescuer last night, takes me home and doesn't take advantage of me. Only to pull me in his office to lecture me about the pitfalls of leading a fast, loose lifestyle. *Well, he is my boss, but where does he get off?*

My memories are cloudy, my mouth suddenly dry. I know why he's talking this way, and the truth seems inescapable; the ugly facts of *what* and most probably *whom*.

The word *shalava* comes to me. The voice is not KomDiv Sobchak. It is Dragunov, I think it is, but I'm too fuzzy to be sure. One thing I do know is that Vlad was right; I didn't know what men were capable of. No such innocence remains now after training.

It also validates Jon's lecture, but I can't tell Jon about Dragunov or my entire cover will be blown. I can only shake my head and say, "No, I ... I guess it was a dream, seemed so real." I trail off.

Jon had been right about that lifestyle catching up with me, and now he's right about something else; I really am becoming quite a good liar. I hear Jon sigh, and I relax a little. "You need to be more careful. This is a wild city, and not everything is as nice as it seems. Drinking to excess is not only unbecoming; it is downright dangerous. What would have happened to you if I hadn't come along."

"I have been drunk many nights." As soon as I say it, I regret it. Jon's expression darkens and he regards me silently. I feel like a child caught doing something wrong.

Finally, he breaks the silence. "I don't think the fact that you've been drunk on many occasions is something to brag about."

Silence. More silence. Jon doesn't know that silence is something I can do all day and all night long. I lived months in complete silence; he is a lightweight in this department. I am nagged by the idea that he thinks he can boss me around and lecture to me like I'm a child.

It feels like we've been sitting here staring at each other for a long time. My mind begins to wander; I think about where I used to play when I was young, the feeling of the breeze on my face – cold, crisp . . . clean. I can almost smell Mamma's biscuits, hear Papa's grumbling and see that secret smile he reserved only for me.

I so want to go home. I am so alone here. My gaze lowers in spite of my stoic façade. I want to go back to my home in Omsk. I feel moisture on my cheek and snap up looking at Jon horrified. He sees the tears and silently hands me a box of tissues. He probably thinks I'm shamed by my behavior, and in a way I am. My parents would be horrified with what I have become. We are simple, hardworking Russians; our family has been in Siberia for as long as I can remember. I can never return to that life; I am truly dead to them. That's why I drink; I have nothing else.

I grasp this American life, because it's all I have. And, I don't really have that either. At any moment, my handlers can end my existence. With a simple swipe of the pen, KomDiv Sobchak can send out the KGB dogs to slaughter me and not just me. They will end my family – Mamma, Papa, Vlad, Gregory, even distant cousins if they can find them. My nightmare rears its ugly head, a specter that haunts me.

"I don't mean to make you cry, Lexy. I just want you to think about what you're doing. I care about you, and I don't want to see you get hurt." Jon is now sitting next to me. *When did he move?* I must do a better job of keeping up with the external world. People just move around and suddenly they're right next to you. I look up into his eyes.

"You care about me?" It is a stupid question from the depths of my desperation. *Is there anybody left who cares about me?* I swallow my sob and retreat into silence. I am still looking at him, and see the ghost of a smile crossing his lips.

"Yes, of course." He takes my hands in his. "I want you to promise me that you will back off on the binge drinking until all hours of the night. I know you're young, but you have to exercise some sort of sense. Promise me?"

In this moment, I would promise him anything. *Oh my, what just happened? Am I this desperate?* He cares about me; somebody cares about me again. There is a connection between us. I feel it, and I know he feels it too. It's probably sexual; everything between men and women has sexual undertones, but there's also something else – an answer, maybe, to my desperate loneliness. "Yes, I promise."

"Good." He lets my hand go and the connection is cut, but I can still feel it. His hands are warm, loving and gentle. I loved feeling his hands, and I reach out and touch his hand again. He doesn't move them. He is still . . . waiting.

"Thank you, sir."

He covers my tentative hand with his own as if claiming me.

Our gaze is locked. I want him to kiss me, and he wants to kiss me. I know it. Or I am more desperate than I think. He licks his lips, and I lick mine in return. Yes, he wants to kiss me. I am back with Ivanna – silent communication between two distressed people, well, one distraught person. I need that contact if only to wash away last night. I am not only shalava. I am not only a dirty slut, drunk and spy for Mother Russia. I am a person in my own right.

"Go back to work." Jon whispers releasing my hands. "I will talk with you later, Lexy. Okay?"

"Yes, sir." My voice sounds meek in my ears; I hear it; I feel it.

Tears. I need to escape this office, this moment in time when so much passed between us. He is the man in my vision; the far away man who rescues me from the monsters. I have known him all my life, incarnated in difference forms but always with those beautiful, caring green eyes. My visions led me to America, to him – and my life will never be the same again. I must figure out a way to get away from Mother Russia. I must save my family, and I have no idea how I'm going to do any of that.

**

Vivian hands me a cup of tea as I leave Jon's office, ignoring my pinkish nose and red rimmed eyes. She makes no comment although she knows I've been crying. She is a strange woman; a shark one minute and a friendly, tea giving ally in the next moment. I smile at her gratefully and return to my desk. I wonder how much she knows about what Jon wanted to talk to me about, but I don't have the guts to ask.

I spend the rest of the morning working hard on the variety of busybody work that newly hired people get stuck with. I don't want to reflect too much on what happened last night or the somewhat embarrassing lecture this morning.

All I wanted to do was go out and have some All-American fun, blow off some steam as the Americans are always saying. Now, I've not only been taken home by my boss, but raped by my handler while I was in an intoxicated state, a state that I get lectured about the next morning by my boss who happens to be the man I love and dream of living the rest of my life with.

I get up to go for another cup of tea. Caffeine and aspirin is the elixir of life for a nighttime party girl. The irony that I'm Russian and can't hold my liquor doesn't escape me. I have never been able to hold my liquor – vodka which is supposed to be running in my veins knocks me out and turns me into a near comatose wreck with a huge hangover the next day. All the water in the world does little to offset that fact. Of course, my parents weren't the typical, drunk Russians; they never drank much either.

"Would you like to go to lunch?" I hear Jon's voice before I see him. Where did he come from so suddenly? I've got to stop living in my head, I'm wary. Is he going to lecture me some more?

His presence seems to suck the surrounding sounds away. It's as if it is just Jon and me suddenly. I jump, regain my composure and turn towards him. His eyes are so pretty. *They're supposed to be the windows to your soul, right? Who said that – Shakespeare, DaVinci? Oh, who cares.*

"I, uh," I splutter.

"I'd like to take you out for lunch so that we can talk some more," *Oh, no, not more about the drinking.* I have survived KGB torture, so why is this man's talking to me having such an effect on me? *Probably, because you've loved him all your life, so what he says matters.*

"Do we have to talk about the whole drinking fiasco again?" I blurt it out softly before I can stop myself.

Jon smiles and chuckles in return. "No, I think you understand my views on that."

Something has changed between us. "Yes, then. Should I bring my steno pad to take notes?" *Good. Keep him guessing about my feelings. Don't appear too forward.* Find out who said that quote. It will keep your mind off his lips and other body parts.

"Of course," he replies smiling,. "I believe you need to get a handle on the duties as my personal assistant."

I wonder if it includes making out. *Squelch that thought. I am supposed to seduce you, though.* That will be fun. "What time is convenient?" I stare at his lips crushing the desire to lick my mine. His lips look so kissable. "1:00?"

"That would be perfect." He turns and walks back towards his office. I am aware of other people around me then, curiosity in their raised eyebrows and soft whispers. *I could care less what you think of me. I have a mission to finish, and I won't be put to death because you people think I act unseemly. Wow! These sharks had already gotten to me. Calm down.* I don't want to give my anger away to them. *Remember, Lexy, you have had much worse in the Kremlin Spy Academy* -- my nickname for the training school. I look at the office staff silently from the kitchen area. *After Sobchak, you may think you are sharks, but you are rybka, small fish in a very large ocean.*

CHAPTER SIX

"The doctrine of the immortality of the soul has more threat than comfort."-- Mason Cooley

September 1963

"Lunch?" I smile when I hear his voice looking up from my desk. We have gotten much closer since that night when I was drunk and he brought me home. I look up at him smiling from my desk which is piled high with reports to type, notes and steno pads. Another typical day in the office. I go to lunch with Jon, and when I come back the sharks are circling. So far, I've been lucky; they haven't found anything out about me that will give them the ammunition they need to take me out. Thank you, Mother Russia for your excellent if brutal training.

"Of course, I was waiting for you to invite me." My voice is soft; I have seldom raised my voice since coming to America.

On the rare occasion when my temper has gotten the best of

my sanity, I have gone straight to ballistic: screaming, snarling and sniping at the target of my anger usually Dragunov. It has never ended well. I smile up at him batting my eyelashes.

The State and my mother gave me wavy blonde hair, flirty long lashes and with the right amount of mascara I've enhanced them even more. My lipstick is kissably flawless, red hot and all the rage for the day, and my dress just clingy enough to be sexy without appearing slutty. I finish the look with three inch heels, black patent leather . . . shiny.

I know the sharks are watching, frowning – biding their time to strike. Vivian, who put me "in my place" on my first day and gave me tea on the day I was lectured, is back to being my enemy almost sneering as I pass, her face drawn up under the black, horn-rimmed glasses. *She hates me now, and I don't care.*

Jon is smiling, and I might get enough information that I can supplement with material from the Free Library to ward off my real enemy – Dragunov. Fortunately for me, Dragunov and my country seem incapable of realizing that you can find almost anything about anything in American libraries. Add a bit of sauce from Jon's conversations – just enough for authenticity and you've got state secrets to share.

The better I get to know Jon, the stronger my feelings, the less Mother Russia gets from me of use. It's a dangerous game, a tightrope that I walk, but I have found the man in my visions, my dream man . . . and I won't betray him. I won't; I can't.

I know my decision probably means my eventual demise in some dark, dank gulag, but I don't have it in me to hurt him. He is the first man save my father who has ever been nice to me. The village boys were nice, but they wanted sex. Sobchak and Dragunov were never nice, and then there was Jon. Tall, strong, Fibonacci beautiful.

"You're daydreaming again." That's what he calls it, and as always, in that tolerant almost loving tone he uses. He is accustomed now to my mind wandering away. "What do you think about when you go away like that?"

I so wish I could tell you, Jon. My heart aches that I must lie to you. But, you have no idea the lengths I go to protect you. "Just dreaming about home, fields of snow covered crops in winter, the crisp air on my face. Little things I remember, like Mamma's soup, her biscuits that were so delicious when hot, my Papa – " I stop. I might have gone too far, revealed too much. I look at him again, and I see the smile on his face.

"We should visit your family someday." *I wish I could, but they are dead to me.*

"We can't. They're all dead." I look back at the steno pad in front of me. *My heart hurts. I want to cry. I will never see them again.* I shuffle some papers to take my mind off of my family. "What time, Jon?"

"What time for what?" I hear the confusion in his tone. He wants to ask me what happened to them. I can't tell him they're being held hostage in Russia. I must make up another lie.

Lies and more lies. Nobody told me I would feel this way about the man I was lying to everyday, who trusted me and took me into his confidence. It was almost too much, and I want to escape. Lies to Jon; lies to Dragunov; lies about my family. *Everything is just dust, dirt and lies.*

"Lunch." I can't say anymore lest the crack in my voice give me away. He can't hear the pain I feel; it will make him want to probe. I can't get him suspicious. I must get myself together.

"Oh, right. One-ish like usual?" I know you are concerned about me. I shouldn't have said they were dead; that was wrong. I need to correct that. You caught me off guard with your humanity. I am not used to kindness.

"That's fine." I nod continuing to push the papers around. I grab my steno book and read the notes I've recorded. Professionalism. *Ignore him. If you look at him, you will dissolve, and you can't dissolve. Remember your training. Remember Sobchak.*

***

"Steak and baked potato, fixing on the side. Can I have a baked potato with my steak. Loaded garlic potatoes with my steak. Steak, steak, steak." I tease him, "don't you know anything else besides steak and potatoes?" Laughing with him is so nice; it is a wonderful connection between us. I can forget my real life for a while and relax.

"Well, it's better than that bird food you eat all the time. Don't you ever eat anything of substance?" It's true. I do eat light, but I have to. I can't turn into a full figured Russian woman on him. Most unattractive.

"It is healthy." My lips curl upwards and I take a bite from a cucumber slice. In reality, I don't care about healthy or unhealthy actually. I could be dead at any moment, so who cares if my diet is hale and hearty. My real reason is that I must stay small, lithe and graceful. Attractiveness is another weapon I possess. Yes, I am crazy for potatoes; I would love a steak, a big dessert preferably all chocolate and a fattening side dish to go with the potato. But, I just can't afford to balloon up. So, I sit here famished, eating bird food and smiling.

"My family is not dead." I let the statement drop into the middle of our lunch, and Jon gets quiet – his gaze steady and his look expectant. "We are estranged, that's all. They were heartbroken that I didn't marry a hometown boy." That was actually true, and if there's one thing I've learned is that you tell the truth whenever you can, because you can't lie about everything and keep it straight in your head.

"I see," he waits again expectant.

"When I elected to come to Washington, they felt I had dishonored them. I would destroy myself. I was never able to get them to believe otherwise." I went back to picking at the salad more to cover my nervousness than anything. *Will you accept my explanation or will you demand clarification?*

"Maybe, one day, we'll be able to meet so that they know you are doing well. I think most parents just want their kids to do well in life."

You don't have my parents – one is a psychotic rapist who will take advantage of any opportunity and another a despot abuser of women and children. My parents are Mother Russia who would kill me in an instant with no more thought about it than cutting off a toenail.

"Yeah, I guess." I trail off not wanting to stay on this subject for too long. Sobchak's image is once again at the forefront of my mind – nasty, smelly, leering old man who gets his jollies raping children. *Would Jon want to meet my parents if he knew they held my real family hostage threatening to kill them if I deviate from the plan to betray him and all that he stands for?*

Jon smiles at me trying to reassure me that most parents aren't that bad. I smile back, but I know he sees the sadness in my eyes, the look of a defeated person staring back at him. "You like your bird food?" I know what he's doing; putting some distance between us and an obviously painful subject. I go along with it, because I want the subject to change as well.

I look across the restaurant seeing a man sitting near the window sipping what I assume is coffee. He is looking at me, and he's not Dragunov. He nods slightly in my direction taking another sip from his cup. It is a signal – *I am watching you*. If anything could reinforce my feelings of being threatened at all times, his slight nod is enough. I look back at my salad, my appetite gone. Every part of my life is monitored. I act free, but I will never be free. I look up again, just in time to realize that Jon is watching me.

What is he thinking; he looks like he wants to ask me a question. "What?" I smile at him; a smile I don't feel.

"I wonder sometimes what you're really thinking. You can go from being laughing, girlish and happy to a woman who seems a lot older than her years, haunted by a specter I can't quite fathom. Sometimes, you seem on the verge of tears, but you always pull back. I get the impression sometimes, that you really don't trust anybody." He takes another bite of his potato – butter, salt and pepper toppings that taste oh so good. I lick my lips. He's still watching me. "Then sometimes you seem to be ready to jump my bones."

"What?" *What did that phrase mean. Jump his bones?* I never learned that part of English. "I don't understand." My throat tightens. It is probably a phrase that all Americans know, and I don't know it. My breathing quickens. I see the question in his eyes. *Why don't I know this phrase?*

He chuckles. "You really are from the Midwest. Haven't you ever heard the phrase 'jump my bones'??"

It is a regional and not a universally American idiom. "I am from the Midwest, yes." I giggle with relief. I play with the ends of my blonde hair, pushing it back behind my ears and over my shoulder. Flirting, distraction, deception. I lean in towards him. "What does it mean?"

After a pause where I begin to think he won't share the explanation with me, he leans close and whispers, "It means make love to me."

Oh, that phrase I know and understand. Having sex. Making out. Make love not war. Lust after your body. Getting a blow job. Doing the nasty. Having sex. "I see."

"That's all you have say?"

Obviously, I need to say something else although what

escapes me. I run through all the American phrases I learned that were comparable to jumping his bones for a second time looking for something suitable. "Well, sometimes I do want to have sex with you. You are a very attractive man."

He sits back in his chair, an amused look on his face, his eyebrows raised slightly. "Well, you are nothing if not honest.

Perhaps I said too much. Wrong phrase, maybe? I bite into a tomato. I really am beginning to hate salad. "Did I say the wrong thing?"

"No, I'm just not used to a woman being so honest."

"I like honesty; it cuts out misunderstandings. We are having a conversation about doing the nasty, correct? You want to get a blow job, perhaps?" I watch him choke on the water he's just swallowed, his face turning an odd shade of pink. I have obviously said too much, but how do I walk it back. "I'm sorry I was just joking." Americans always chalk a faux pas up to joking.

He starts laughing so hard that he holds his side chortling, tears running down his face. I start laughing, too. My laughter is more to blend in with the situation than a feeling of humor on my part. *I have no damned idea what was wrong with what I said*, but I learned that if I found myself in a situation like this, to do as the Romans do in Rome. Go with the flow, I believe it is called. My understanding of American men is that they always want to get blow jobs. But, I believe you didn't expect me to say that right out, did you? Better to make it a joke than to have him think I have lost my mind, inhibition and my sense of propriety.

"You are amazing," he says finally regaining his composure. "I never would have suspected that you would say something like that."

"Well, you started it with that bone jumping joke. I just figured I would continue the joke." Bat your lashes, look innocent girl. Smile sweetly. Does he have an erection? He sure looks hard. Nah, my imagination.

"Okay, I think we'd better leave it there for now." I watch as he covers his lap with his napkin. *He does have an erection.*

We finish lunch and start back towards the office, What's so nice about our relationship is that we can joke around and be friends. My parents were friends. I think the basis of any good, long-term relationship is the ability to be good friends, and the better I get to know Jon, the more I love him. I don't tell him that, yet. I am just happy to have him as a friend.

I shouldn't use the word long-term either. But I can hope. I don't believe in God, but sometimes, just sometimes, I wish I did. It would help me delude myself into believing that I stand a chance to become Jon's lover, confidant and lifelong friend.

In reality, I know that is impossible and that my days are numbered.

***

Dragunov is increasingly impatient with me and dissatisfied with the tidbits I keep tossing him, so I must come up with a big lie to tell him that will satisfy him. *What would make him happy?*

"I think he may have something to do with organized crime," I say, intimating that Jon is in league with the mafia even though my true suspicion is that he's trying to figure out how to get them out of the country and out of the government. It's better that Dragunov think Senator Caine might be duplicitous, because that's something we could use against him, to blackmail or otherwise control him or even destroy him if necessary.

So this keeps Dragunov hopeful despite the continuous lack of hard information on him from me.

"Our time is running out, Aleksandra," he says to me one during one late-night meeting in my apartment. "And our patience."

I know he means his patience and Sobchak's. And I know

what that means for me and for Dragunov as well.

Death.

"I'm getting closer, you have to admit," I say. "If we can tie Caine up with these mobsters, we can make him do whatever we want. We'll have him right in our back pockets."

Dragunov steps toward me slowly, menacing, glaring at me. "So you keep saying. But until we have hard evidence, we have nothing. You have nothing."

"You'll have it, Dragunov, in due time. You can't rush these things."

"Now is the time when results are due, you fool! There are other factors at play which are contingent upon you doing what you were sent to do. They are not for you to know, but they cannot wait for your personal time table."

What other factors are at play?

He stares at me, scowling, silence wrapped around him like a burial shroud. Finally, he lights a cigarette, and blows the cloud of smoke into my face. It burns my eyes, the inside of my nostrils, my throat quickly dry and scratched.

"You know what will happen to you, to your family if you fail. Your father will not die well."

I know his mind.

I will kill you one day. Soon, my dear comrade. "I am going to leave to go back to work on completing my mission, if that's okay with you."

He stares at me with that wan expression, sickly countenance – I hate you more than I hate Sobchak. You are the product of his depravity, and you spread it over me like a cancer to choke out my life and leave me desolate, violated and alone. Don't you think I know what you are? Sobchak is driven by his decadent desires, but I think you are motivated by cold rage that has choked your soul out of existence. You are a shell of a man; you have not one redeeming quality. I look at you and all I see is evil, coiled and waiting to spring. I look at you and all I see is a man I will one day kill.

"I need you to recognize the seriousness of our mission." Dragunov pulled at his tie. "This is not something we can play around with.

You think I'm playing? Well, yes I am playing a very dangerous game. But, I intend to win it, and not lose my cool. I must leave you before do what I want -- wrap my hands around your scrawny little neck, before I take that stupid, skinny tie you wear flattened on your stark white shirt, under the slightly frayed, always dark suit jacket and use it as a garrote to strangle the life out of you. It would be messy, I know, and likely traceable – hemorrhaging in the eyes are a dead giveaway that you met an untimely end, but it would be worth it rather than continuing to listen to your stupid threats and needless intimidation.

"I do recognize the dangers of messing up. I know that failure is not an option, comrade." My lips curl, my eyes open wider. Yes, I feign innocence and use all the other techniques I learned. *I will even flirt with you if that's what it takes to make you believe me for now.* After the KGB training, there isn't much I won't do, even keep quiet about how you raped me in my sleep, how you stuffed your nasty penis down my throat, how you jumped on top of me like the humping chimpanzee that you are, thrusting your hard, stiff penis in and out until you gained release.

"I really do understand you, Dmitry." Leaning forward, I can almost feel your breath on my cheek. The smell of you disgusts me; my stomach turns, but I do it anyway.

"Don't you think I know what my life is worth if I fail at this? Don't you think I understand with brutal, unflinching clarity, that the Zolotov family from Siberia will be no more – that the KGB will hunt down and kill anybody remotely related to you?"

"I don't understand why you feel the need to punctuate my terror with constant reminders of my vulnerability." I whisper.

You are an evil, frightened little worm, and I could crush you beneath my three inch, staccato heels if I wanted to.

"I just want you to be very clear about things. I know that your family is small, but they are still your family. And you know what will happen to them if you fail."

You have no regard for my family save beating me over the head with their impending demise. You don't care about them; you don't care about me. Why do you pretend to, when we both know you will strike without mercy, report back to Sobchak that I have failed and order the execution of those I hold dear? You don't know about anybody else except my immediate family. Mother Russia isn't as omniscient as she thinks. My other relatives have long fled, when they first heard I was going to be a spy. You must think me an idiot.

"Dmitry, I know we are in a real spot if we don't get this accomplished. We must work together as a team and trust each other or we will both fail. And we both know what that means." I smile at him, my stomach churning. *Hopefully, you don't see the disgust behind my gaze, or my smile that is the smile of your eventual demise. I will really smile when I kill you, Dragunov.*

"Very well," he stands to leave my apartment. "I think this is going to work out, and we will both bring honor to our families and to Mother Russia."

I stand almost at attention. Serious. Straight face. "To Mother Russia." I don't crack a smile, and I carefully school my tone so there is no hint of sarcasm to give me away. *I hate Mother Russia and all she stands for.*

Dragunov looks at me for a moment before responding, "To Mother Russia and the success of our mission." I watch him turn and leave my apartment, pulling on his overcoat and placing his black Fedora on his head as he walks out.

One day. One day I will repay both you and Mother Russia for all your kindness.

***

I'm getting to know Jon Caine's mind as well. He's authoritative with his staff but never abusive. I see why Vivian puts her hand to her chest every time she sees him or talks about him. His strength makes him someone to respect, but his fairness and kindness make him someone to admire; while his sheer charisma and handsomeness make him someone to desire.

He's funny but never inspired with the need to impress. He's charming in an easy-going way. But there is a power simmering underneath, like lava always threatening to burst up through the surface, scalding and dangerous.

Trying to manipulate this man isn't easy.

And it's very dangerous.

I know the lobbyists behind the waste disposal contracts are associated with organized crime. Everybody knows. Jon himself once said, "Damn gangsters are gonna take over Washington, if we don't keep 'em trapped out there in the swamps."

"Louisiana?"

"New Jersey. I hate the idea of them doing business at all, but I think there's a way to..." He trails off, and then smiles. "Anyway, that's politics."

"You don't want to tell me."

"It's for your own protection, Lexy."

"But I'm your personal assistant and, well, your friend... I hope."

He smiles, reaching out to touch my chin, the gentle caress of his fingertips sending ripples of excited pleasure down my neck to my quickening heart. *He is so gorgeous, so sexy. Stop, Lexy. Remember your mission.*

But he doesn't crack.

And I don't give up. I let the days pass, keeping an eye on Jon and on the various members of his staff. And they seem to be keeping an eye on me. One day I'm walking down the hall and Dan Oglvy steps out of a room right in front of me. I stop, catching my breath.

"Oh, excuse me, Mr. Oglvy -- " But he just glares at me, not saying a word. "I ... I was just on my way to get some copies made for the senator."

Again, not a word. His unmoving face wasn't lacking in emotion; he seems to be choking back his anger, all his energy coiled up and ready to spring out at me. I half-expect his hands to jut up and grab my throat without warning.

Does he know? I wonder. *Why doesn't he turn me in?* Maybe he only suspects. Is he waiting for me to slip up, giving me enough rope to hang myself? Maybe there's some personal tension, like I have with Myron (and like everybody has with Myron)?

I can only stand speculating as Dan blocks the hallway, his broad, brawny physique an impassible obstacle.

"Lexy," Jon calls as he comes down the hallway behind Dan, "you have those copies?"

I nod, then glance at Dan, who slowly considers me. He

looks at me, at the papers in my hands, then slowly steps back into the little office he slid out of to block me in the first place.

Jon says, "You okay, Dan?"

Dan fades into the office as I step up to Jon, lifting the papers to him. "Here are those waste management reports, three copies each."

Jon looks at Dan, seeming to mull over his Chief of Staff's odd behavior. He says, "Thanks, Lexy," as he takes the papers, his mind on Dan's quiet tension as he turns and heads back toward his office.

I follow him.

I had thought to make a copy of the waste management report for myself, to turn over to Dragunov, but I know that's too risky. If a stashed copy were found anywhere after I'd been sent to make the copies, I'd be caught red-handed.

So I sit quietly in the bullpen while Senator Caine takes a meeting with Dan and Myron, each armed with a copy of the report.

I'm not allowed into the meeting, but my hope is to swipe Senator Caine's copy of the report as soon as I can.

A call comes in and, with little else to do, I answer it. I don't recognize the voice on the other end of the phone, but he speaks in a thick, Italian/American accent, with blunted consonants and mumbled turns of phrase.

"Who's d'is?"

"I'm Aleksandra Tomanek, the senator's personal assistant."

After a brief pause, the man says, "Ten o'clock, tell him to come alone." After a click, a buzz tells me the call is over. I hang up and look around the room; everyone going about their business without a clue as to what has just happened. Even I'm not sure, and I'm the one who took the call.

After Jon's meeting, I invite myself into his office to give him the message. I have to be delicate here. I'm worried for Jon's safety, but I know that whatever is going on, there is certain to be a lot more to it than I realize. I'll have to go along with things and be able to strategize on the spot, based on whatever the newest information is, if any.

And I still want that report.

Because I still have my mission, I am less and less enthused about it, but I still need to get that report to Dragunov. It is something he won't be interested in; state secrets are juicer items, but it will prove once again that I am on the job.

I'm still trying to figure out how to keep Senator Jon Caine, out of the pocket of the KGB. But I'm not convinced he's doing anything in the wrong that would put him there. Of course, I can't tell them that, or he and I may both wind up dead. So I have to protect Jon from himself, from his enemies, from my enemies and from me.

I decide to move forward cautiously and maximize whatever opportunities arise, on whichever side of the fence they happen to spring up.

I say, "You had a phone call during the meeting, they left a message."

"Who was it?"

"He didn't say; just ten o'clock, and that you should come alone." Jon sits back, his face going pale. I can tell it isn't good news. "Jon, what's happening here? I know you want to protect me, but as your assistant, isn't it my job to try to protect you?"

"No," Jon says, "it's to assist me."

"What about as your friend?"

Jon smiles and so do I. We really are friends.

And those KGB mind control techniques really do work.

Jon says, "Things are getting complicated, things I can't even explain to certain members of my staff." Jon looks around his office. "Things we shouldn't even be discussing here. Have you had lunch?"

I barely have time to shake my head before he and I are hustling through the bullpen. I can feel Vivian glare at me and Deloris, too. They're both jealous of me, and they're both in love with Jon. I know that.

But they're no threat to me or my efforts to get close to Jon, whether for the KGB's purposes or my own, which are quickly becoming two very different things.

Walking quickly through the streets of Washington, Jon explains, "Cars could be bugged too. We have to be really careful here."

"We?"

He looks at me and nods. *I've won his trust.*

He says, "I've been trying to get the mafia to believe they're getting a great deal. With these contracts, they'll have enough control to feel like they've succeeded. And that'll keep 'em out of the federal arena, which means I've succeeded."

I recognize the technique from Sobchak's class, a detail I neglect to introduce into the conversation. Instead, I let Jon speak as we walk past a filthy man sitting huddled on the sidewalk.

Jon stops and stoops to him, pulling a few bills out of his pocket and handing them to him. "Get something to eat, partner." He stands and we move on, my body flush with admiration for him and attraction *to* him.

Jon says, "Anyway, now they want to have a meeting, probably to discuss terms."

"And you can't meet in public," I say. "They can't come to you; you can't just stop into one of their joints. Even phone calls and letters are out."

"That's right. But it also gives them the upper-hand. They work best in secret, that's their strength."

As I know only too well. It's the same mentality that governs the decisions of big government and small back in Siberia, and even more so in the rest of the Russian empire.

Jon says, "And if they think I've double-crossed them, I won't be coming back from the meeting."

I look around with new concern. "And you can't tell anyone or arrange to have them there to back you up."

"Exactly. I hate having to meet secretly with these dirtbags, but it's the only way I can see that'll keep them out of Washington. They're fighting to survive, like everybody else. And I won't have them slipping their people into the senate, the house, or even... I don't dare say it."

"The presidency?" I finish his sentence.

"It's bad enough, what's going on with Kennedy and his so-called connections. I'm going to stop it where I can before it spreads like a cancer and brings the whole government down."

I can hardly believe I'm saying this, but I do ask, "Aren't their more... legal ways to shut them out?"

Jon chuckles, looking both ways before leading me across the street. "We've been trying those for decades, that's why we're in this mess now."

We get to the restaurant and Jon nods at the owner, who ushers us to a table in the corner. "Then what are you going to do?"

Jon shrugs, taking the napkin off the table and laying it across his lap. "I'm going to the meeting."

"But Jon -- "

"Look, chances are I'll be fine. If they whack me, they lose their big contract, I think they know that."

"What's to stop them from just doing business with somebody else?"

"Lexy, I'm a U.S. Senator. If I just disappear, that's not going to be so easy to cover up. And it'll make approaching any other senator or getting any real business done next to impossible for them." After a tense moment, he adds, "Of course, they do have their ways."

A waiter brings us two glasses of water, but I'm too nervous to drink. The waiter asks Jon, "The usual, Senator?"

"For me, please." Jon looks at me, and I look up at the waiter.

"Caesar salad and some minestrone soup, please."

The waiter nods and steps away.

I sit on the other side of our little table trying to figure things out.

I don't want them to kill him, I reason. He's such a good man, such a waste of life is incomprehensible, especially if I can stop it. Can I pit Dragunov and his resources against the mafia and somehow pull Jon free of the crossfire? Wouldn't that satisfy Dragunov's agenda and my own? But how do I do this without tipping Jon off to my connections and, thus, my true intentions?

And if I do manage to pit the KGB against the mafia, Jon and I would be right in the center of a massive war that we'd never be able to outrun.

There must be another way.

I say, "You'll be taking that little car of yours," I say. "You can't have your driver sitting in the limo while you have this clandestine meeting, right?"

"Afraid so."

"Shouldn't you have it checked out? Did you say it might be bugged?" Jon considers it for a moment, nodding. I add, "But couldn't a bug have been placed there by someone on your staff?"

"An inside job?"

I shrug. "Who else could get close enough to you? And you know *I'm* not involved, I only just started working here recently -- "

"Long after this whole mess started," Jon says, "that's for sure. Then again, you could be a member of the mob, working undercover."

I sit in the tense silence, not knowing what to say. My stomach sinks with a cold dread, my lips go slack.

Then Jon breaks out laughing and shaking his head. "As if, right?"

I laugh too, nervously. "Yeah, good joke. Hey, fuh-get-aboud-it!" It was my best Italian mobster imitation, and I already know it is pretty bad. I giggle as he looks at me. It probably sounded more Russian than Italian.

We both chuckle together as the waiter brings our food – his delicious, mouth-watering meal and my rabbit food. Might as well be kibble for all that I care. One day I will be able to throw this salad at someone and have a real meal. I stab a cucumber and smile in spite of myself.

After lunch, Jon has me look through his VW for a device of any kind, and there isn't one. Yet, I drive the car back to my apartment to retrieve a small, long-wave transmitter, a homing device. Dragunov had given me the bug, along with other various implements, to use when the time was right.

I intended to plant the device on the car. But I need to be there when all this goes down. I need to see that Jon's all right, to be able to help him if possible. And there's no way I'm going to be able to convince him that I followed him without a car of my own.

The only way is to plant the homing device on myself and then stash myself inside the car.

In the trunk.

But first I have to talk to Dragunov.

He's not in his own apartment, so I wait for him to arrive. I know he's monitoring me, and for me to drive up to my own apartment, alone in the senator's car, is bound to attract him. My only hope is that it happens in time, because if I'm gone from the senator's office too long that will arouse suspicion. And if Jon goes down to that parking structure to find me and his car missing, it'll raise a lot more than suspicion.

It'll raise the body count.

Finally, Dragunov arrives and I begin to set my trap.

"He's in league with the mafia," I tell Dragunov, "there is no doubt. He's got a secret meeting with them, in fact. If you can surveil the meeting, record it, you'll have everything you need to make the senator do whatever you wish; you'll have total control over him."

Dragunov nods. "When and where?"

"Use the homing device," I say, "it's already planted in his car. But these men, they may try to kill the senator. If he dies, you'll have nothing, the entire mission will be a loss. So collect your secret gunman, the spies you have scurrying around spying on me, and have them ready to take out the senator's enemies if necessary. We need him alive, is that understood?"

Dragunov smiles, almost in disbelief. "You're asking me if I understand. Reconsider your position, Aleksandra. I'm still in charge here."

"Then take charge and get it done. And one more thing; you'll need to make it look like a rival gang, in case there's any shooting. So bring something along you can leave at the scene."

"Like what?" Dragunov asks. "I have no idea what rivals these men may have, or -- "

"Do you want Sobchak to hang us both up by our ankles?" My voice snaps with anger and impatience, and I let it. It confuses Dragunov, and that is one of Sobchak's own strategies of mind control. "You find a way and make it happen. I shouldn't even have to be explaining these things to you, Dmitry," I slur his American name, a clear insult.

And he takes it. He doesn't have a choice.

I push past him with, "Now I've got to get back to the senator's office before he realizes I've been missing. Don't screw it up, Dragunov." I slam the door behind me.

I stop on the way and have a copy of the car key made, and get back to the office. Everybody's busy with their phone calls and their typing; nobody seems to notice how long I've been gone.

Until Nathan says, "Where've you been?" I turn to see his smiling, chubby face. He adds, "...All my life?"

I give him a forgiving chuckle to hide my relief and walk toward Jon's office. I feel Dan's icy stare clinging to me as I go down the hall, Myron shaking his head in disgust.

In the office, I set Jon's keys on the desk. "I ... I won't ask where you're going, but... just be careful, okay?"

Jon looks up from his desk with a warm smile. He says, "Lexy, if I don't come back -- "

"You will," I insist, "you will come back!"

"I know, sure I will, but just in case I don't, don't come back to this office. Get out of town as quickly as you can." He stands and steps around the desk to take my hand. "You have enemies here, Lexy. If any of them are working against me, you'll be the next one to fall."

I allow the fear to show on my face, knowing that they all have as much to fear from me as I do from them, maybe much more. But I also know that there may be a lot going on that I don't know about; machinations that could include Dan, Myron and perhaps others in the office.

Betrayal is a double-edged sword.

So it isn't without some legitimate sense of concern that I step out of the office and down the hall, back among my enemies.

At about four-thirty, I ask Jon if I can leave early, citing certain women's issues, and he allows it. There's nothing more I can do for him.

As far as he knows.

I use my new key to pop the trunk and climb in, pulling it closed behind me without clicking it shut. I jam a rolled-up stack of paper into the latch and hold the hood in place.

I have five hours to spend waiting in the trunk of that little car, but it isn't more than a few minutes before Jon himself climbs into the driver's seat, starts the engine and pulls out. I rock and sway in the little trunk, barely enough air to breathe, my stomach already turning with motion sickness.

I'm grateful for the time when the car is still, parked in front of his townhouse, no doubt. I'm sorely tempted to crack the hood for some fresh air and a peek around, but I know it's too risky. So I stay in my pitch-black cocoon, lungs straining behind my compressed ribcage. I manage to get some sleep, but wake up once the car jostles round me again. After another brief journey; I know we're on our way to the meeting.

We park and are idle for some time before I hear Jon's car door open and close. He's sitting in the driver's seat, I realize, waiting. He's early, wants to ensure against an ambush. Smart.

And good for us, I realize, that gives Dragunov and his men time to close in and take position.

I'm in the trunk during the entire thing. But from what I can make out of the action outside, there is a brief conversation, Jon's voice almost audible. I'm sure that Dragunov is close by, long-range mics picking up the conversation. I hope that Jon isn't saying anything too indiscrete.

No, he's smarter than that. What's Dragunov really likely to get out of this? Worry about that later depending on who walks away from this alive.

If anyone.

Then I hear the voices get a bit louder. One man shouts. It sounds like Jon, but I can't be sure. Gunshots ring out, loud and echoing. My body twitches with every shot, knowing an errant bullet could plunge into the car and splatter me all over the inside of the trunk. I also know that Jon is much more likely to be killed than I am. The quick burst of gunfire ends as suddenly as it began. Tires squeal as footsteps pepper the area around the car.

I push the hood up and peer out of the trunk of the car, to see Jon standing in the center of a parking lot near an old dock warehouse. He holds a gun, and in his shock and confusion, he turns it on me. I raise my hands. "Don't shoot! It's just me, it's Lexy; don't shoot!"

He reaches down and pulls me out of the trunk. "Lexy, what the hell are you doing here?"

"I'm sorry, I stowed away," I say, having worked out beforehand what I'm going to say. "I was worried about you, wanted to help."

He looks me over; no gun, no rifle, not even a crowbar. "How were you going to help?" *Great, he's angry with me.* "Hiding in the trunk is one of the stupidest moves I can think of, short of jumping out of the trunk blasting away with a machine gun and killing everyone including me."

I stammer a bit. I haven't thought of that. I shrug and say, "I thought ... I guess I wasn't thinking."

Sirens were dim in the distance but getting louder fast. "No, you didn't think, and you could have been killed." Now he's worried and angry. Maybe this wasn't one of my brightest plans, but I am new to the spy business. Who knew that hiding in the trunk could get you shot or yelled at, because he's definitely yelling at me, and I don't like it.

"Let's just get outta here," he says, climbing into the driver's seat while I get into the passenger side. He pulls out with a skid and tears away from the scene.

"What happened?" I ask, concealing my well-educated guess.

"Don't know, not sure," Jon says. "Double-cross; they sandbagged me, must have known I was playing 'em for a bunch of suckers. But, you shouldn't have been here."

"And you shot them all?" I ignore the chastisement, and instead concentrate on him and his gun bulge in his jacket.

"Not a single one," Jon says. "There were others, hard to say where they were shooting from; experts, for sure, military, maybe." *Dragonuv.*

"But, who could have known about this meeting? I'm here, and I didn't even know where it was going to be."

Jon considers as he cranks the wheel, the car swaying around us. "Somebody from my staff, I think; Dan or Myron, maybe both."

"Frankly, I don't trust either one."

"This is Washington, Lexy, you really shouldn't be trusting anybody."

"I trust you," I said, automatically and not premeditated. *Did I just say that?*

I see his lips curl upwards in a small smile. I relax. He's cooling off. "I know. I trust you, too."

"Don't be mad at me, Jon," I said. "I was only trying to help you, if I could." Little do you know that I risked exposure with Dragunov to keep you safe. If he knew my real feelings for you, I would be dead.

"It was a stupid move. You have to think about the consequences of your actions, Lexy." *Great, he's still angry.*

I change the subject, "Could it have been a rival gang? Maybe, they followed *them* to the spot and not you at all."

"Maybe," Jon says, gazing out the window and then up into his rearview mirror. "I did sort of think I was being followed, but... I dunno, maybe you're right. Time will tell, I guess."

I look at him, the gravity of our situation swelling to fill the little car. "How much time?"

Jon tries to smile, but he can't fake it. He knows that there may be precious little time left for either of us.

He says, "Whoever it was, they didn't want me dead, so that rules out a double-cross from inside the office. But until I find out who did do that shooting, I better stay out of sight; you too, I'm afraid."

"Stay... out of sight?"

"Just for a day or so, until we see what kind of media coverage there is, have Deloris issue a press release if that becomes necessary. Hopefully, the cops and the press won't link this massacre to me. We'll have to play it by ear." He turns to me with a smile, this one melancholy but legitimate. "Ever been to Connecticut?"

CHAPTER SEVEN

"Love never dies a natural death. It dies because we don't know how to replenish its source. It dies of blindness and errors and betrayals. It dies of illness and wounds; it dies of weariness, of witherings, of tarnishings." -- Anaïs Nin

October 1963

We drive for two hours to the lovely state of Connecticut, but it is pitch black as we drive through those winding country roads. The beauty of the scenery is not lost on us. Even hours after being set up for death and barely surviving, by circumstances he can't fully understand or explain, Jon is still considerate, caring, and interested.

He asks me about my family life, my brothers --Vick and Greg, as I describe my Wisconsin kin. He's so genuinely interested that I hate lying to him.

But neither one of us can afford for me to tell him the truth, of course.

And he has no reason to lie to me. So when the conversation turns to his life's story, it rings with a special poignancy, his innocence lending it a somber quality.

"She wanted to take me for everything," he says, "and then just a bit more."

"Even after she was cheating on you?" Since, in my country, she'd run the risk life imprisonment for such behavior, it really did strike me as odd and, as it should anybody, unacceptable.

"That was where she went wrong," Jon says. He turns, imagining the good times they had, the love they shared when good things went wrong for them both, together, as they so often do. "Anyway," Jon adds, "it is only love."

"Love doesn't have to end in pain," I say, not sure if I believe it myself. But I think back to my own parents, how they clung to each other for strength as I departed, keeping each other alive in the face of insufferable sorrow.

I am surprised when Jon takes my hand. It stops the recollections, the dream I run from, and it's replaced by a warm feeling in my stomach. He says nothing and neither do I. We are friends, and hope springs eternal in me that he might want to be more. The signs and connection has certainly been there. And if blatant jealousy from others is any indicator, we might be headed into a relationship.

When we get to the hotel, I suggest he let me go in and get the room. "You're a U.S. senator," I remind him. "And we want to stay out of sight, remember?"

A few minutes later, he's surprised that I've only gotten us one room. "How can you protect me if I'm in another room?" I ask my eyes wide and innocent, my lips pouting and vulnerable. "It has two double beds."

He smiles, his face unreadable. I wonder if he's still angry with me, or if the promise of something more has distracted him from wanting to protect me and failing.

We retire to our room, dark making it difficult to make out the accoutraments. It doesn't matter, thought because the air is thick with sexual anticipation that surrounds us as much as the darkness. Neither of us reaches for the light.

We are the light, I think, but I don't make the first move. I can't. American men who let women do that are pussy-whipped. The colloquialism comes to mind unbidden. It is also true with Russian men. *Some things are universal.*

We stand in the stillness of our pent-up attraction, every

little movement amplified. I can sense his body near to mine; feel his warmth, the tiny sounds of his clothes as they shift on his tall, muscular frame echoing in my ears. I can smell him, cologne and manliness make a heady brew.

He is only inches from me, moving as if in slow motion. We both are near to stillness as the moment stretches out ahead of us, the certainty of our eventual union rolling up upon us like a giant wave, pulling back the sea to gather its forces for an irresistible blow.

"You are too young for me," he whispers finally breaking the stillness.

You have no idea how old Mother Russia has made me, I think. If you knew that your vision and my love for that mystery man of my dreams is the only thing I had to hold on to when Sobchak was making me obedient and compliant, you wouldn't hesitate for a moment. I was yours before I ever met you. You saved my life; you protected my soul. I owe you everything.

"Oh, hell," he says finally breaking the silent stay between us. He takes me in his arms, pulling me to him, lifting me up on my tiptoes. The wave breaks, much like the foamy flecks of water breaking against the shore, and we are swept away in the passion freed at last. Our lips meet, his tongue pushing into me, passionate, determined and insistent like a twisting, wet whirlwind. We pull away after what I think is a long, languorous kiss, his breath hot against my face, our chins caressing, cheeks and foreheads rubbing in a sensual celebration of their long-awaited embrace.

"You are a child compared to me," he whispers, as if by saying it aloud will stay his passion.

"I am not as young as I look," I reply, because sadly I am not. Mother Russia has made me old before my time.

"Yes, you are. I am 14 years older than you," he says, slowing. *No, don't stop.*

"Age means nothing to me," I reply, perhaps too quickly, "besides, older men always love younger women. It is normal."

He chuckles softly. "You are sweet." It takes everything in me to not push this forward. I know I need to wait, but I also know that if he backs off, this will be my end. I reach up and caress his cheek, slowly making my way down to his neck, then down his chest. I feel a tiny gasp, then a sigh. I gently rub his chest, carefully rubbing his nipples. *Men are sensitive, too.*

"You know what you're getting into," he says, caressing me in return. "If we do this, there's no turning back."

I don't want to go back; I want you. "Yes, I want this," I whisper, "please."

He begins to caress me in earnest, strong hands that follow the curves of my body; the smooth arc of my hips leading upward to my narrow waist and then, higher still. My heart beats faster as his fingers find the bottoms of my breasts; tips gently tracing the supple curves, the outer rims, the firmness and fullness. I have never felt this way when having sex; rape isn't sex so how could I. This man wants to 'make love' to me, and I want him to.

For so long, I have felt that sex was a tool to be wielded for the good of the State. I never cared, letting Sobchak train my body while my mind went elsewhere. He would attack me, rape me, beat me. He never cared about me, and during those sessions, my mind would go home to where my parents dwelled or to my vision of a man I'd never met, a man I fell in love with even though he didn't exist.

Sobchak would be spewing party nonsense, spitting, his stench foul, his face a vision of horrid obesity, and I would feel my mama's hands gently brushing my hair into place. Sobchak would force me to look at him, and I would see my papa's smile, his warm gaze on me and I would really be home. He would lean against me, rubbing to arouse himself, and I would feel the chill of fall in Siberia walking through the forest.

And, during the worst sessions, I would be at a ball, moving in the arms of my dream lover, laughing and free. *How could I not love you?*

My body responds to his hands, answering their queries, rewarding their explorations. My fingers wrap around the lapel of his jacket, pushing the garment back over those massive shoulders and down to fall to the floor behind him.

His necktie is already loosened and is soon removed, the buttons of his dress shirt holding on for dear life as I peel the white cotton away from his firm, hairless chest.

We kiss again, tongues even more engaged, inspired by greater urgency and commitment. He pulls my dress up over my head, the air suddenly cool on my skin as I undo my bra and toss it aside.

We fall onto the bed kissing each other as if we've known each other forever. At least, that's how I feel, and as he kisses his way down my neck, goosebumps rising along the backs of my arms and around my nipples, my chest heaving as my breath becomes deeper, stronger, harder. My body quivers with anticipation, blood pounding, juices stirring until they are spilling over, soaking my panties until Jon pulls them down and off my legs, freeing me.

Freeing us both.

"I have wanted you to do this since the first time we met."

Since before we met, but I can't tell him that. I feel, rather than see him smile down at me.

"Yes."

"If I'd known that, I might have moved faster. I didn't think you'd go for a guy in his 30s."

"I'm not," I reply. "I go for you, and I didn't think about your age."

He laughs then. "You are so unfiltered, Lexy." I giggle in return. It's not a meditated giggle, but a real one that bubbles up from before the time I went to the KGB.

"Your wish is my command," he leans in and starts to kiss me again, and we are both swept away in the passion of the moment and a commitment to the future. I know that if I survive, this will be the man I spend the rest of my life with. *I have looked for you for so long, Jon Caine.*

***

The next morning is a flurry of phone calls for Jon. I know I should contact Dragunov; he could be thinking any number of wild things, and there's no reason to rattle the dragon's cage. I need to get to the pay phone in the lobby, and slipping out just isn't that easy. I tried to leave once, and it turns into us both having room service. I don't dare try to combine the phone call with a bathroom visit for fear of getting caught. I need Jon to be at least one flight of stairs away when I call Dragunov.

And there is much to be learned in the meantime. Jon says, "No, Dan, I'm fine... She's with me... "

Jon works the whole thing like a master. And, I have to admit, so do I.

The television reports a mob shootout with evidence found at the scene, the dead body of a low-level mafia grunt.

Dragunov, I think to myself. I didn't mean that kind of evidence.

But that's Dragunov, Sobchak and the whole KGB; ruthless and deadly, willing to end a life for the mere convenience of it.

No mention is made of the senator's involvement in the shooting at all, and as far as everyone at the office know he's just grabbing a little time away to clear his head.

My only concern now is Dragunov. How upset is he? Did he get anything he can use on Jon? Was he shot or killed?

That would be too much to ask for, but I also know it won't matter. There's always going to be another to take his place, one who could be even worse and more dangerous still. *The monster you know . . .*

I wait until Jon is on the phone again, this time with Deloris, contriving a statement on the recent gangland violence threatening the city. I say, "I'm going down to the gift shop for a pack of gum."

Jon looks over. "Hold on, I'll go with you."

"Oh come on, it's just a pack of gum. I'll be back in five minutes. Want anything?"

Jon considers it, and I can hear Deloris' voice on the other end of the phone. He looks at me and says, "No, I'm fine. Thanks. Hurry back."

I nod and exit as he turns his attention back to the phone. *He wants to protect me.* It's so sweet, I go downstairs with a smile on my face.

I use the pay phone in the lobby to call Dragunov's local phone number. He answers on the first ring and I say, "Dmitry, it's me."

"Well, well, if it isn't Aleksandra Capone."

"I'm glad you're all right, brother." I allow myself an accusatory tone when I add, "I saw that you covered your tracks."

"In your service, sister. Our papa would like a word with

you about it. He's quite distraught."

"I warned you it could go that way. Didn't you get anything of value first? Photographs, surely."

"Only from the back, nothing conclusive. Nothing was said of any value either. Where are you now, sister? Let me come and take you home."

I know what he means by that, the deadly subtext. And my own life is not the only one at stake.

"I'll be home soon enough. And I look forward to telling Papa that I did as I was supposed to do, but that you were the one who failed to collect the hard evidence we needed. It is you who failed the family, brother, not I."

I know as soon as I say it, that this is an unwise strategy. It only pits Dragunov against me, the most likely scapegoat to bear the brunt of his failure. When the phone clicks and the buzz returns, I'm filled with dread; my blood running cold, skin tingling. As always when the stress goes through the roof of me, I want a drink, maybe, many drinks to quiet my inner demons – fear and loathing.

I walk past the gift shop, stopping and doubling back for the pack of gum. I'm in a daze as I buy it, my mind flashing with grim images of gunfire, the imagined face of Dragunov as he looms above me, choking me to death to protect his own miserable life.

I see other images; buildings burning, prison doors slamming shut. My own momma and papa stand over a grave, heads low over their stooped shoulders.

My grave?

I can't make out the name on the headstone. The agony of this curse of mine, this so-called gift, is the uncertainty, the lack of clarity. I know something is happening, or will happen, but I never seem to have enough information to be able to stop it.

On the way back from the store I hear somebody say, "See? A body like that!"

I stop and turn. There is an open bar in the lobby, where five people sit around a table; three women and two men, all barely in their twenties. One of the women, a redhead, reaches out and shakes her head. "I didn't mean to offend you, honey, I was just saying I wish I had a body like yours."

I give it a little thought. "I guess it'd be pretty hard to be offended by that."

One of the men stands; he's tall, young and good-looking, with a preppy haircut and dimples. He extends his hand and says, "Robert. Have a drink with us, so we know you're not put-off."

I check my watch. "At eleven in the morning?"

They all look at each other. One of the other women, a pretty brunette, says, "We're on vacation."

The other man, chubby and smiling, says, "Hey, it must be five o'clock somewhere!"

They all chuckle, Robert coaxing me toward their table.

Who are these people? Are they really just guests of the hotel? Odd that they'd approach me, of all people. My body's not so much greater than the redhead's, not such that she'd make that big a deal about it.

Flattery, I recall, one of the basic and most potent mind control methods. Could these people be KGB operatives? American spies, maybe? They could have been following me for weeks. *Or, they could just be on vacation, Lexy. Stop being so paranoid.*

I decide to take him up the invitation. If they are KGB, I might be able to figure that out if I talk with them for a while – a slip of the tongue, a slight accent undetectable to Americans. If they're Americans, well, I'm the rival of any young spy. I can handle this. And if they're just chatty tourists as they appear, then what's the harm? There might be some worthwhile information to extract from them, and it could be fun. I have never had the experience of just hanging out and having American type fun when I was drinking to excess. This might be a new feeling. *And, who cares. I'm probably dead anyway when Dragunov catches up with me. Might as well have some fun.*

What about Jon? Another part of my mind pipes up, I'll just have one drink and leave. What harm can that do. I wonder if Jon would come and get me? Does he really care, or does he just want me for sex? That's all I'm good for, anyways.

I shrug off the thoughts and order a Bloody Mary, tangy and spicy and peppery on my tongue. I can seduce a man, but put me in a group, and I need a drink to start talking even if it's all lies. Robert introduces his friends as Maggie (the redhead), Joanne (the brunette), Sally (the other woman, a chubby blonde) and Mike (the skinny one). They're all very pleasant and chatty and claim to be from Harvard University in Cambridge, away for the weekend.

"Wait 'til President Kennedy gets going," Mike is saying. "you'll be seeing some big changes." They love their President. Idolize him almost. It is an odd feeling that they look up to their president and revere him without coercion.

Maggie waves him off, taking a sip of her margarita. "Who

cares about politics? Did you see *West Side Story?* Amazing! I'll bet it wins all those awards this year." The fact that they don't want to talk about politics is refreshing. They are my age, and they don't care about anything too serious.

"Those awards are meaningless," Robert says. "That's just a way to increase everybody's salaries. Anyway, best movie this year is *The Apartment."*

Joanne turns to me. "What about you, Lexy? You a movie buff?" I have seen neither movie. In actuality, I have never been to the movies, so I can't really tell you if I like them or not. Entertainment wasn't a big part of my KGB training to come here and be a spy.

I shake my head. "I guess music is a bit more my thing." I finish the Bloody Mary and order a Cosmopolitan. I love Cosmos.

"Who do you like?" Robert asks.

"Um, I think Patsy Cline is great. *I Fall To Pieces...*" I had heard this song on the ride up to Connecticut, realizing how out of touch I was with simple things. Too much focus on something isn't the best thing either. I pray they don't ask me for any other song by Cline.

"That is good," Maggie says. "I think she's gonna be around

a long, long time."

I don't understand these people. If they're KGB, they're very good. If not, they're very dull.

Robert says to me, "I don't see a ring on that finger. Are you here with somebody special?"

Wait a minute, there may just be something going on here after all. *How much should I disclose? Are they just clarifying who I am so they can carry out the hit on the senator, probably me as well?* Or are they going to kidnap me, as the senator has been concerned might happen all along?

I say, "No, um, it's just me for the weekend. I'm... getting away from the big city for a while. I go to school in Boston."

"Really, B.U.?"

"You guessed it, Maggie."

"You're just across the Charles. We should get together sometime. I'd love to show you around the campus." Robert smiles at me, sexy and confident. His eyes dilate as he leans closer to me. *Ah, he wants to have sex with me. Harmless.*

Family must be rich. He hasn't lived long enough to have that much confidence in himself alone. I smile at him, not wanting to encourage him, but not wanting to brush him off entirely. *Remember, you just made love with Jon, and he is your dream come true. It's just innocent fun,* my wild mind puts in.

"Y'know, it's not the 1950s anymore, it's the 60s! We're in the modern era now. It's time to start casting aside the old taboos, wouldn't you say?"

Yes, you want to 'jump my bones', I think to myself. He's not that bad looking and he's giving off all the right signals. *What about Jon?* I lean back and away from Robert. I look at Maggie blushing and realize my assertion is right. *Okay, does every American male only want sex?* This would be boring if it wasn't laughable. I don't want to have sex with Robert, even though he is telegraphing his available status.

What about Jon? I think. He won't come get me. If there's one thing I have learned is that men are men, no matter where you are. Jon has had sex with me, and now he's on the phone doing business, so why would he care about what I was doing?

"Is that why you all came here, for an orgy?" I ask. They're jaws drop, shocked by my frankness, and then burst out laughing. They share knowing glances, nod and shake their heads, chuckling and shrugging. But they don't deny it.

"Lexy," Jon voice is behind me and my heart sinks and swells simultaneously. *Oh, he did come. Oh no, he's mad again.* Grabbing my arm, he pulls me to my feet, "Let's go."

"Jon," I say. "I was just -- "

"I thought you said you were here alone?" Robert asks, clearly confused, and looking from Jon to me, I can see him calculating – he's outmatched.

"You said you were going down for a pack of gum," Jon says softly in my ear. "not go drinking and talking to a bunch of college kids about an orgy."

Jon pulls me away, his fingers digging into my arm. "Ouch, you're hurting me," I try to end it civilly with my college friends. "I am actually here with somebody, although I didn't realize we were this close." I laugh as Jon starts to drag me away from the table. "I don't think he'd be interested in the orgy anyway."

Robert and Mike stand. Chivalry to the fore. Great. "I think you better leave her alone, pal," Mike says.

"Stand down, son," Jon says, pulling me away from the bar. "Didn't you hear her say that we're together." I nod yes, and they back down. Jon doesn't say a word until we're back up in the room.

But that doesn't stop me. "I was only having a couple of drinks and some fun. They offered, what harm could it do?"

Once in the room, Jon barks, "What the hell is the matter with you?"

"Like I said, it was just a couple drinks."

"You don't know those people! They could have been mafia, or... who knows?"

I shrug. "I don't think they were mafia." How can I tell Jon, that I'm about to die and nobody cares, not even me.

"And you say that based on what? How much do you know about the mafia?" He looks at me anger still visible in his furrowed brow and downturned lips.

I am conflicted. I am so used to no one caring about me that his obvious attention to my welfare is unnerving. "Nothing," I stammer, "it's just a hunch, but I think they're Harvard students."

"And how did you arrive at that conclusion?"

"Because they said they were going to Harvard, and they wanted to have sex with me. They weren't exactly subtle." I snap back sarcastically.

"Lexy, right now we don't know who our enemies are. They could offer sex or an orgy to get you alone. They may not be mafia, but they could be from another senator's staff, or even the KGB."

"I sleep with you once, and now you're running me around like you own me*?" I don't think so. I don't care what my mission is. I have a right to have some fun.* "Besides, I like drinking even if it's 11:30 in the morning.

"We've talked about your excess drinking issues," his voice gets quiet. "I don't want you drunk at 11:30 in the morning."

"It was two drinks." I didn't want to admit that it would have led to a lot more drinks had he not interfered. *So what, I like drinking.* "I can drink and go to an orgy if I want to. I'm a grown woman."

Jon looks incredulous. "Then, why don't you act like one? I'm trying to protect you, protect us…. And, you're ready to have sex with the first clown that comes along?"

"I don't have sex with clowns," I snap. "And, no I hadn't planned on having sex with them. It was just an invitation."

"Do you have any idea how ridiculous that sounds? I'm trying to protect you."

"I don't need your protection, Jon Caine. I can take care of myself." *I'm probably already dead, and nobody cares – not even me.*

"No you can't." His green eyes flash when he's angry, and he looks so beautiful . . . so sexy. I push that thought away. "Not from mobsters, gangs and generally nasty people." That brings me up short. I hate to say it, but he's actually right. Last night, we had been on the run. And, this morning I'm making friends with drunks and orgy goers.

America is just so damned confusing – loose and easy, tight and conservative. And you never know where the enemies are. In Russia, it was easy to tell who your enemy is. They were usually armed, stinking old men who leer at you; they started getting old when they were Dragunov's age. They have rotten teeth, drink-soaked eyes and they smell vaguely like death incarnate. They like to fuck children, and they like to torture trainees into frightened, silent submission. In America, everything is different – the home of the free, the land of the brave…. You never know what the hell is going on.

"I... I never thought about it like that." For me, the only hostile country is Russia, but it could be another country like Cuba or Korea. I really hadn't thought about it.

"That's the problem, you didn't think!" His voice is sharp with an angry ring, each word feeling like a slap across my face.

"That's a fine thing to say! I'm the only one in the office who thought enough of you to follow you to that meeting." *And got Dragonuv to intervene to your benefit.*

"You were the one who took that call, Lexy, the only one who knew. And, in terms of following me, hiding in the trunk was a stupid, childish thing to do. If they had shot at the car, you would be dead."

I glare at him defiant, and he stares me down. After a minute, I lower my gaze to the floor. After a pause, I continue, "So, now you think what? I'm too stupid to help you out if things go wrong?" I state the obvious, hiding in plain sight.

The silence is thick between us, before he shakes his head and waves me off like an errant child. "What were you going to do if things went south? Beat the mobsters to death with the tire iron in my trunk? I don't think you're stupid; I think you're reckless. You don't stop and think, you just act and react. You were in way over your head, and if that rival gang hadn't attacked, I couldn't have protected you. I would never forgive myself if something happened to you, Lexy."

You don't know what the hell you're talking about, I want to say. Mister Big-Time Fancy-Ass Senator who knows everything; did you know that you're in bed with a KGB spy? I could cut your throat here in Connecticut and be back on a plane to a hero's welcome in Moscow before sundown. Talk about in over your head. Talk about not thinking.

Even as I think it, I know it's a lie. There's no way I could ever kill this man. Quite the contrary, I will probably wind up dying to protect him. And there it is, that niggling feeling in the pit of my stomach, radiating outwards and upwards to my heart. *I love you, Jon Caine. I have loved you my entire life in visions and dreams; now, here in the flesh, I can't help but love you more.*

Too late to stop now.

"Well?" He snaps me out of my revere.

"Well what?" What the hell did he just say?

He's moved closer, standing in front of me frustrated and angry, "You can't just run around willy-nilly like a child hanging out with the first group of people who come along. This isn't child's play. It's the mob, and they will kill you."

He looks at me for another moment and his gaze turns thoughtful, "But you are barely an adult, more a child than an adult, aren't you?" He rubs his chin with his hand, and I wonder what he's thinking. "You must not do that again, Lexy."

You sound like Papa after the time I got lost in the forest for a day. When he saw me, it was a combination of relief and fury. I had never made him that angry before or scared him that much. Jon has that same look.

"I am not a child." I counter suddenly. "And, I can do anything I damn well please."

"No, you can't Lexy, and if I have to treat you like a child to protect you, then that's what I'll do. I care that much about you."

I'm stunned, but before I can act, Jon grabs my hand pulling me towards the bed. In one swift motion, he sits down on the bed and pulls me over his lap, slapping me hard on the butt with his bare hand. The sting shoots through my cheeks, clenching beneath his flattened palm. "Don't you ever wander away from me again; do you understand?" After several more slaps, he repeats, "Do you understand?"

I sob, "Yes, I understand," I thought it was a rhetorical question.

"You are stubborn, selfish brat, and you will get us both killed with your bullheadedness." He punctuates each word with a slap to the point where I'm willing to agree that the sky is chartreuse just to get him to stop. *This is beyond embarrassing. How will I ever look him in the eye again.* I guess I really scared him and that makes me feel worse. *He does care about me. It's one helluva way to show it.* I try to remember my tactics for disabling someone, but all I can think about is that my bottom is on fire, and that I'm in this situation because he does care. I start crying in earnest, but he isn't slowing. "I am so disappointed in your behavior. You don't think and you're going to get yourself hurt or killed."

I can't believe he's doing this. I plotted to kill Sobchak when he whipped me in that cold, dank place he called the reeducation chamber. Hatred is a powerful painkiller, but with Jon I don't have hatred. I love him and every smack, every word is all the more painful because of it. *I don't want to be a brat, and I don't want to get us killed.*

"I won't do it again." I wail, my face red as I grip the side of the bed.

He stops spanking me finally and sits me up, looking in my eyes, serious and angry. "You are so foolish sometimes. Even if those kids weren't our enemies, think of what they'd do to you if I hadn't intervened. Did you want to have sex with them?"

I try to look away, but he's holding my chin and I can't look down, out the window, up at the ceiling – anywhere to get away from his concerned look. "No," I whisper. "I guess I don't really care what happens to me sometimes. Nobody has cared about me for so long." Tears flow from me as I desperately try to get them stopped, not so much from the spanking but more from my own feelings of desolation and despair "I am so alone. You never could understand what I feel."

"Then, make me understand, baby," he says. "I thought we had the start of something special. I haven't felt this way about a woman in such a long time. What is it that you're not telling me? I care so much what happens to you, and not because we slept together. I have cared what happened to you for a long time ever since that night I put you to bed."

"I can't talk about it. It hurts too much," I try to pull away, but he gathers me up and goes and sits at the head of the bed, leaning back on the wall taking me with him.

"You can tell me anything, baby. I will listen and understand. Why do you think so little of yourself? Those guys were offering you drinks, probably drugs and sex. Why did you think that was a good idea?"

"It was just something to do," I reply feeling barren, empty. You don't know me; you don't know anything about me, because if you did, you would hate me and walk away from me.

"Something to do. Jumping off a bridge is something to do, but I wouldn't recommend it."

I sigh, but say nothing. You know why you did it because I wanted to see what he'd do. I wanted to see if he cared enough to stop me. And, he did exactly what I hoped he would do; stop me from destroying myself. I certainly won't tell him that. I also know that I would have drunk in that bar until I passed out. In fact, that had been my intent if he hadn't come, hadn't stopped me.

Win-win. If he didn't show up, I could pass out and get away from the pain inside me for a while. If he did show up, maybe it would diminish the pain I feel all the time. *I want to go home, back to Siberia, back to my family – my brothers, Papa and Mamma.*

I hear him sigh behind me, "You are such an enigma sometimes, Lexy. It's like you're a duck on a pond."

I giggle in spite of myself. "A duck?"

"Yes, you look placid gliding along, all the while you're paddling furiously under the water. There is so much going on under your neutral expression. When I look into your eyes, I sometimes see so much pain and fear. I think it's why you drink, why you put yourself in danger. What are you so afraid of?"

My humor abandons me. He is an American; he has never known oppression, fear and loathing. He lives in the land of the free, and no one will kill him if he makes a mistake. He is also very perceptive which is dangerous to the mission, because if he figures it out, I won't be able to kill him. And, I won't let anyone else like Dragunov kill him either.

What can I say? That one day in spite of his love for me, I will have to return to Mother Russia? That because of my love for him, I will fail in my mission and I will probably die because of that failure, and my family as well? I can't answer his questions without giving it all away, so I simply lean back on him and close my eyes.

"Sometimes you seem so old for your years – melancholy and forlorn – like you've walked through hell to get to where you are. Then at other times, you'll pull some hair brain stunt like you're a child with no knowledge or care in the world. Like earlier. You scared me, and made me so angry with you."

"I'm sorry," And I mean it. "I didn't mean to scare you."

"After last night, even if you wanted to hang out and go drinking with those kids, you should have asked me."

"You would have said no," I reply softly. He laughs at my response.

"That is true. Drinking at 11 in the morning after escaping from the mafia with our lives? I'm not trying to control you; I just want you to use your head. I know you're very smart, but sometimes you just seem to throw your common sense to the four winds. And you seem hell bent on destroying yourself, sometimes." *Four winds?*

"I know," I whisper. "Sometimes, I just don't care. I don't know why." I do know why, but I can't tell him. He holds me tighter.

"I don't want to lose you, Lexy. You have no idea how close I've gotten to you, even before we made this official. I can't just stand by and watch you destroy yourself. I just can't. Even if you can't tell me why, I'll accept that for right now. I would like to know one day everything about you, but I can wait."

I don't respond, and after a few moments, I hear him sigh. Jon is a take-charge kind of a guy, and I know he doesn't like not knowing. I have officially been upgraded in his life, although I'm beginning to realize that I had probably been upgraded long before we came here.

"I will tell you everything one day." I feel his lips kissing the back of my neck. "I will try to think more." He kisses me again.

"Okay," I like sitting with him. His body is warm, comforting; his arms wrapped around me feels wonderful. He still sounds angry, but at least he's holding me.

For a little while, I can be normal. No Mother Russia, no Dragunov, no monsters – just Jon holding me making me feel safe and loved. I fall asleep in his arms and sleep deeply. When I wake up it's dusk, and I'm under the covers warm and safe. I slept all day? I guess in this anonymous hotel room, where even Dragunov can't find me, I could relax.

I look over to see that Jon's watching television engrossed in the news broadcasts, not only of the shoot-out we barely escaped alive, but also of foreign news, in particular events in Cuba.

Cuba. Dragunov alluded to that, didn't he? *There are other factors at play.*

The TV news anchor is saying: "President John Kennedy pledged today that the United States will not intervene militarily in Cuba to overthrow Castro..." Odd that we're here after a falling-out with the mafia, who are known to have a strong presence in Cuba. *Could Jon's interest in the mob have more to do with keeping an eye on Cuba than keeping an eye on New Jersey?*

"Hi" I say from under the comforter. I don't want to get up yet.

"Hi, sleepy head. You slept all afternoon." Jon comes over, and I wrap my arms around him and start kissing his neck, breathing hard and heavy into his ear. *Maybe, we can make love again.*

He gently pushes me away, removing my arms from around

his shoulders. "We are leaving really early tomorrow. I want order room service. Are you hungry?"

"Starving," I reply, sitting up in the bed. "I could eat half a cow."

Jon laughs at me. "Okay, how about a cheeseburger and fries instead."

"Yes, great." All American food. I love it. "Do they have milkshakes?" I love milkshakes, all sweet and cold.

"Yes, I think so. What kind?" I look at him blankly, my mind searching for the right word. "Vanilla, chocolate or strawberry?"

"Vanilla and chocolate and strawberry," I reply slowly.

He laughs again. "Okay." He picks up the phone to call for room service.

"I'm going to take a shower," I tell him as he waits for room service to pick up. He nods okay, and I disappear into the bathroom.

"I need to finish the first draft of my speech for Tuesday's presentation." He shouts after me.

"Okay." I close the bathroom door and turn on the shower

looking in the mirror at myself. I turn and survey my rear end – pinkish. *Great,* I rub my hand over it and it smarts. I wonder if this has changed the nature of our relationship. *Will we be close like we were last night? Does he care about me?* My wild mind answers immediately. *Of course, he cares about you; he just spanked the crap out of you because you put yourself in danger. And, he's still here, although the galaxy only knows why.*

I get into the shower letting the hot water sooth my body finding some nice smelling soap and soaping up the wash rag. It's slightly rough, but it feels good as I rub it across my skin. Hotel showers in good hotels are always a pleasure. What few I've been in – exactly two with the senator – seems to have endless hot water. It is one of many things I love about the United States.

I feel a slight chill, realizing that Jon has opened the door and stepped into the bathroom. "Can I shower with you?" My heart skips a beat. *He still wants me.*

"Yes." He opens the sliding glass door and steps into the shower with me. He takes the rag I'm using and soaps it up into a lather and carefully starts washing me, first the back and then he turns me around. He starts rubbing my chest and when he rubs across my breasts the feeling shoots straight down to my groin. I moan softly which brings a smile to his lips. I feel his interest rising and pushing hard against my stomach. Jon starts kissing me, washing between my legs, caressing me in a way that makes me start panting with need. The water is warm, his hands are gentle and insistent, and I can feel myself being swept up in the power of lust and love. For the moment, I can forget about Dragunov and Sobchak, and simply be the girlfriend of the man I've loved forever.

***

I wake slowly from a dream surprised that is not filled with the horror that is their usual tone. I reach out and feel Jon next to me, his chest rising and falling in a steady rhythm that comforts me. I think back to my dream smiling: I see myself, and Jon, as we lay in that hotel bed. I see him looking down at me as I sleep, smiling. I can almost hear his thoughts, how fond he's becoming of me in spite of, or maybe because of, my stubbornness and willfulness. My fears that they have driven us apart don't hold up under the warm picture of Jon's quiet consideration and ample appreciation. He strokes my hair.

I think I feel his fingers caressing the side of my head, but I can't be sure if the clarity of the vision is convincing my body, or if Jon's touch on my body is in fact directing the visions. When the morning comes, sunlight streaming in through the window, it hardly seems to matter. It's a new day and we're together.

CHAPTER EIGHT

"Nature, in her most dazzling aspects or stupendous parts, is
but the background and theater of the tragedy of man." --
John Morley

Coming home from Connecticut, Jon insists on escorting me
up to my apartment and searching through the place to make
sure nobody's there waiting for me. *Does he know about me?*
Why would he think somebody would be here? Do you think
the mafia would try to kill me? Do you actually suspect I'm in
league with them?

I'm worried about Jon stumbling upon Dragunov, who
would very likely be waiting for me; if not in my room than a
mere floor above.

My apartment is empty, and Jon seems ready to leave.

"Jon..." then trail off to say, "Senator Caine, I..."

"Lexy," he says, approaching me. "It's Jon, now and always." Then he kisses me, our passion spilling over the walls of my worry. Our tides mingle again, powerfully pounding in the craggy rocks of our hardened souls, refreshing them in the salty spray.

Every part of me is alive and tingly. Each of his kisses cause me to moan. Touch me there, kiss me there. He leans down rubbing my nipple as his hand slides down under my shirt while his other hand undoes the button on my skirt. It falls away, then he pulls my blouse and I unbutton it for him. All men everywhere in Russia and America know how to relive a woman of her bra. I think they must learn it about the same time they learn to shave. My bra hits the floor.

He's still kissing me; he's driving me crazy. Aroused is an understatement. I gasp as his hand slides inside my panties, finding me wet, open ready. I reciprocate pulling at his pants. He obliges and the touch of his hands on my waist makes me jerk as it becomes part of the sweet, delicious sensation. I am so alive and horny when he touches me, something I have never felt with any other man. Not even in my humping and grinding youthful explorations have I felt this way. I love the way he takes his time, touching me everywhere, watching and smiling at my reaction then caressing, kissing and teasing me somewhere else.

My stomach feels like it's twisted into knots, and my legs feel like jelly. I have been trained to seduce him; why is he seducing me? His mouth is insistent and hungry against mine; I gasp as his breath tickles my neck. He is pushing my panties down before I know it, and his hands feel cool against the smooth skin of my buttocks. The soreness from yesterday is almost gone, but it's there enough to make this feel like a little pain and a lot of pleasure – salty and sweet.

I want him inside of me, and he is slow and considerate. I am in heaven, sheer bliss at his touch as his fingers stimulate with slow, deliberate circles. Just as I think it can't get any better, he stops rubbing me, picks me up easily and walks towards my bed. I pout because he's stopped but he smiles.

"Patience, baby." he whispers in my ear and then lays me down on the bed.

"I want you inside me." I surprised that I'm whining, but in this moment, I want what I want. He smiles and obliges filling me up and making me complete. We move in sync towards our climax and like yesterday, it's wonderful, heady and satisfying.

He lays down rolling off and out of me, covering me with kisses in the process. "I care so much about you, Lexy, but sometimes you can be really infuriating. I don't want anything to happen to you." He kisses me and looks like he might fall asleep, but after a few minutes he regains himself and rises to go to work. He covers me with the blanket, and kisses me lightly on the lips. "No partying tonight. Get some sleep so you're fresh for work tomorrow. Okay?"

"Okay," I reply. I don't want to argue with him. I want him to stay, but I also know that Dragunov is coming for me, and I need to prepare an ambush to kill him once and for all if necessary; a long kitchen knife is already hidden in the couch cushions.

If he comes at me, I will kill him, knowing that I will need to make up some excuse for Sobchak. I pray that Sobchak will believe that Dragunov attacked me from jealousy, anger or just plain insanity from being in America. Sobchak will send another agent to ghost me, and I will have another excuse to delay him and the onward marching of the boots of Mother Russia.

But when Dragunov finally does arrive, he's surprisingly pleasant. He waves off the shoot-out with the mafia as a mere trifle, the price of doing business. He assures me that he has won me a final chance to prove myself, which I know means that he is still forbidden to kill me.

Sobchak has given me another chance, and Dragunov is more than happy to take credit for it. Maybe he thinks there'll be some carnal reward in it for him, I cannot tell. But I do know that only his frustration will be stoked, today or any other day.

Dragunov doesn't push that point either. He's altogether too reasonable, which I know must be under the threat of death. I know that, for now, he only draws breath because I do, that my death will mean his own.

For now.

I know that won't be long. As the days go on, I try to find things I can give to Dragunov that won't be too damaging to Jon; the restaurant bill, some interpersonal office communications about Jon's speeches and his associations with various lobbyists and pressure groups around Washington. It's all pretty banal stuff, and I can tell Dragunov is getting less and less patient as Sobchak becomes less and less satisfied.

I know Dragunov is ready to kill me, and the fact that he hasn't means Sobchak has forbidden it. But I also know that Sobchak's desire to keep me alive won't last, I can almost feel his heart hardening against me from halfway around the world. Soon his decision will flip, and his desire will be for my part in the mission, and in life, to come to an abrupt end. And when that happens, I feel sure that Jon and perhaps countless others will be eradicated as well.

I've been given one more chance, and I can feel it slipping away. I need to give them something good, very good, or I'm dead. Soon.

November 1963

I have begun to suspect that Dan Oglvy is watching me, suspicious of disappearing lunch receipts and too many quick visits to the photocopy machine. I begin to operate under the constant concern that he'll lurch out from a doorway and stand before me, accusing me with some undeniable proof of my true guilt.

So when I hear someone say, "I know what you're doing," I'm surprised its Myron's snide tenor and not Dan's bombastic baritone.

"Excuse me?"

He smiles and looks me over. "You can't fool me. I know exactly what you're up to."

"I... I don't know what you mean." What I'm up to? I'm working for the Senator. What the hell are you doing?

"Nice try. We all know about your little trip to the country. We all know you're sleeping with him. And we all think you're a vicious, little, gold digging whore."

Before I think, I slap him, the sound echoing through the bullpen, grabbing everyone's attention. I can be a cool, calm and collected spy unless you talk about Jon Caine. Then, I just lose my mind, it seems. *This is not good. I might have just lost my job. Damn.* Myron had been speaking softly, but the slap took the privacy factor out of our conversation, and he is standing in front of me, holding his jaw and gawking. Clearly, that was not the response he was expecting.

"And, if I am sleeping with him like you say, whose business is it of yours?" I hiss at him matching his soft tone. *Be careful, Myron,* I glare at him hoping he can read my mind.

"You slapped me," Myron steps back raising his voice in a high pitched shrill. *This is not going to end well.*

Vivian approaches the two of us, looking first at Myron and then at me. "What's going on?" She is trying to lower the level of hostility.

"She slapped me." Myron implores showing her the red handprint on his face. "She had no right to do that."

"And you had no right to call me a gold digging whore," I snap back softly. "If I am sleeping with Senator Caine, how is that your business? He is a single man, and I'm a single woman. There is no impropriety here unless you make it." *I plan to kill the last person who called me a slut and a whore. Be careful, Myron, you don't know me.*

"You called her a gold digging whore, Myron?" Vivian is speaking rapidly and softly knowing that his screeching is attracting attention. "Are you insane? Lexy is right. It's none of your business." Myron looks wounded, angry. I know he will be an enemy from now on.

"She should know her place," he continues loudly. "How can she come in here and –"

Vivian cuts him off, "I know you want to sleep with him, but he likes women." I am surprised at Vivian's candor, as Myron's cheeks redden.

"I, uh, I don't know what you're talking about," his voice is much lower now.

"Shut up, Myron. It's no secret to me. You've just been lucky that the senator hasn't found out." *Another tidbit to file away for future use.* Myron is a homosexual, and in these times, that's a real problem.

"What's all this?" Jon approaches, looking from Vivian, to Myron to me.

I look behind him and Deloris is behind him heading back to her desk. Obviously, she got Jon when she saw me slap Myron. *To help or destroy me, I wonder.*

"Lexy?" Jon looks at me expectantly. I can either destroy or save Myron's career at this moment, and he knows it. He blanches but says nothing. Vivian is also watching me, not sure which way I'll go. I look away but say nothing.

"Is somebody going to tell me what's going on?" Jon asks the group at this point.

Vivian speaks up at that moment, "There was a little misunderstanding about some paperwork." *Nice cover up, Vivian. Now, I can get you both fired.* Clearly, Vivian knows that if I say what really happened, Myron is gone and she'll be on thin ice for covering for him. She will make a good ally.

"Is that true, Lexy?" Jon looks at me again. I look at Vivian and smile. *I need a powerful ally like her in my corner.*

"Yes," I reply softly, "just a misunderstanding." Jon looks at the red handprint on Myron's face as he turns away trying to hide it from him. Then he looks back at me his eyebrows raised. *We will talk about this later*, is what his expression conveys, and I know this isn't the end of it.

Depending on what happens when Jon walks away will determine what I tell him later. Myron, faggot that he is, might be useful to me. *So, you're in love with the senator, too*, I think, but I say nothing.

Jon says, "I see. Very well." His voice is dead quiet; his eyes all green and stormy watching me. He knows something more than a misunderstanding has occurred, but no one is talking about it. He is ready to protect me, and my heart cinches with that knowledge.

In actuality, I want to leap, twirl and dance like I used to in the forest of my homeland. Jon is in many ways like my papa but a whole lot sexier. *You marry the first man you love, right?* Jon turns to head wordlessly down the hall toward his office, and the din and hum of the usual activity slowly returns to the bullpen. Vivian approaches me cautiously.

"No one has a right to speak to you like that," she whispers to me. Clearly, she has picked sides, and she has become my ally.

"Thank you for coming to my rescue," I speak softly. "I didn't mean to slap him; he just caught me totally off guard." *That much was true. Had I been ready for his nastiness, I might have controlled my temper.*

"Jon has been a very lonely man since his first wife died. It's about time he found some happiness," I look at Vivian anew. There is sadness there, an unspoken yearning. *You're in love with him too.*

Vivian turns and walks toward her desk. I have much to think about, and I also need to think of what lie I am going to tell Jon. I know if I tell him the truth, he will fire Myron and probably Vivian, too. In spite of my training, and perhaps because of it, I don't want that to happen to Vivian. While I don't care a fig about Myron, I think I have come to care for Vivian Galbraith.

***

That night, Jon takes me to dinner at one of his favorite places, darkly lit and secluded. The salad is delicious; I'm growing quite used to it and even think about becoming a vegetarian.

"You'll need a good source of protein. Hope you're fond of beans." He has given in to my bird food diet choices. We start talking about politics, which almost everybody in Washington talks about. It seems almost mandatory.

"Do you see yourself running for office someday?"

I shake my head no, as I give it some thought. "The whole business just seems so crooked to me. Present company accepted, of course."

Jon chuckles and shrugs. "Nobody's entirely honest in politics, or they'd never survive."

"Well, I guess that's true. But it's not how I want to live." I ignore the irony of my own half-truth. While I know damn well that I'm living a life based on lies and deceit, it's truly not the life I *want* to live.

"At the moment," Jon says, "you don't really have a choice."

"What's that supposed to mean?" I ask, allowing myself to appear more upset than I am. It's another mind-control device, using pre-emptive emotion to effect a person's decision-making. "Like I'm not smart enough to make my own decisions? Why, because I'm a woman?"

"No. it is because you're so young."

"Is that so? Well, you're not that much older than I am."

"I'm in my thirties; I think I know what I'm talking about a little bit more than you do."

I let myself sneer at him, enjoying the role of perturbed American liberal. "You think you do, but you've got another think coming. There are big things happening in this country, Jon. With Kennedy, you're going to see big changes; among races, even among genders. It's not the 1950s anymore." I used almost verbatim what the college students had said in Connecticut.

"And so much the better for it," Jon replies.

"We women have had the right to vote for a long time now. It won't be long until we're paid the same as men in the workplace, too."

Jon considers it, and then shakes his head. "There you reveal your naiveté, the whole weakness of your starry-eyed optimism. I think it will be decades before women are paid the same as men; even for the same hours, same job, same everything. I don't agree with that either. It's just that until a woman makes it into the highest office in the land, as well as key positions right under that, can any legislation change. And, that doesn't even count major corporations who still have two different pay scales and roads to success."

"And why's that? Because, we don't deserve it?"

"I didn't say that. Lexy," My tone is defiant and sulky. *I want him to agree that things will change now.*

"I don't mind having these little chats with you, but I won't have you putting words into my mouth, and I won't have you taking this tone with me." Jon is patient, quiet in response to my tone. *I hate that. I want to fight with him and win the argument. Decades!*

"Taking this tone?" I repeat ignoring the deteriorating mood of the evening. "I'm a grown woman, with First Amendment rights, thank you very much. I'll say what I like in whatever tone that pleases me. Unless you think women don't deserve equal rights any more than they do equal pay?"

He raises his eyebrows surprised. "If it is my company, there would be no such restrictions. Men and women would be able to rise to the level of their abilities with equal compensation for a job well done. But, that's not what I'm talking about. And, no. I don't like your tone."

By this time, I can feel the eyes of every woman in the room, their conversations hushed as they watch our exchange. The rebel in me decides to really play it up. *Oh stop, before you really make him angry.* I ignore the warning.

Jon is glaring at me, but says nothing more. I have to win this argument, one side of me thinks. Why? The other side puts in. Are you crazy? Remember what happened the last time you made him really angry.

"Don't you glare at me, with your brooding silence and your threatening stares."

"I have never threatened you, Lexy," he says softly. "Why do you think that?"

I don't know. My whole life is threatened all the time? I say nothing letting the silence stretch out between us. I glare at him until I can't any longer. I look at my hands wondering what to do next.

"I don't like you right now," I hear myself say. *Now, where in the hell did that come from?*

"Why? Why are you so angry, Lexy?" I look up into his beautiful green gaze and I want to melt. He is just so gorgeous, and I think he really wants to know. I can't tell him my rage is for Mother Russia, Sobchak and Dragunov. I can't tell him that.

"I was just expressing my opinion, and you wouldn't listen to me." *What am I? Five?*

He continues to stare at me silently waiting for me to continue. Silent expectation. To me, it's just another tool, and the fact that he's using it just makes me angry all over again. I try to stare him down, but silence doesn't work as a defense against itself, especially when everybody in the room is waiting to hear what you have to say.

"I've never threatened you nor given you any reason to feel threatened, Aleksandra. We have talked about this before." *He's using my full name. That's not good.* The rebel in me screams 'so what' and I continue.

"Of course you have, that's all you men *can* do; threaten and bully and push your way around, here in Washington more so than anywhere. It's your stock in trade! Well, I'm a woman, and I'm a citizen of the United States of America, and I will not be quieted any longer. Someday this country is going to wake up to the inequality that's ripping us apart. I just hope by that time that it isn't too late, that people like you haven't destroyed the very democratic concepts that this great nation was founded on." I have no idea what I'm shouting, but it sounds good. I have no idea why I'm shouting at him either when I really want to scream at Sobchak. Jon has done nothing but be loving and kind to me, and I give him nothing but a headache. *But, I can't stop.*

I stand, drop my napkin on the table and dump Jon's wine in his lap, storming out of the restaurant.

I guess I just showed you who is boss. The rational part of me quips softly, *what have you done? He is going to be livid.* The scene with Myron comes back to mind, and I slow, wondering if I've just ruined my mission, and more importantly, have I just murdered my relationship with the man I love dearly and passionately.

I'm jump in a cab before I can think about it anymore heading back to my place. Damn, that was stupid, Lexy. Why do you always lose control with him? Dumping wine in his lap? Are you crazy?

I walk in my apartment, tossing my purse on the coffee table in the living room, and stepping out of my heels. Why do I do that? Maybe, because I feel safe with him. Maybe because I hope. Maybe, I just know that on the day he finds out I'm a spy, he will hate me, so why wait for that shoe to drop. I'm getting better with these American colloquialisms.

I hear a key in the door and the door opening. *Where can I hide?* I look around swiftly, running to the small closet in my bedroom, opening it and crawling inside. *This is ridiculous.* I pull the door closed and sit dead still. He's walking around in the living room. *Crap, I know he sees my purse and my shoes. He knows I'm here somewhere.* I hear him walking into the bedroom, then into my bathroom, then back out into the bedroom. I know it's him by his footfall. *What do I do? Hiding in the closet is stupid. But I know he's livid. Maybe, he will cool off in one or ten years. I had to throw the wine on him.* I hear him open the top drawer; pulling out sweatpants I assume. We each have two drawers in each other's apartment. I hear the drawer close. I am almost holding my breath as I hear the footsteps come closer to the closet I'm hiding in.

What do I say if he finds me? I was looking for something so I climbed in the closet to find it and closed the door behind me? He is stopped in front of the closet door. He swings the closet door open, looking inside at me. I look back at him trying to think of something to say. He pulls me out of the closet, and towards the living room.

I don't even have time to scream before he's upon me, a flash and a force of pure fury. "Don't kill me," I squeak as he grabs me by my shoulders. I start shaking and can't stop.

He slows for a moment, and I can see his surprise. "I'm not

going to kill you, Lexy. I would never hurt you. I keep telling you that, but actions have consequences and your behavior tonight was atrocious and childish." He drags me into my small kitchen grabbing one of the straight back kitchen chairs.

"No," I suddenly know what he's going to do, and I want no parts of it. "You can't." I try to twist away from him, but he's too strong.

The spanking in Connecticut pops back in my mind, and my cheeks redden with embarrassment. He pulls out one of my kitchen chairs, flips me over his lap and pins me with his legs and hands. My dress goes up, my panties go down, and I feel the first of many smacks on my rear end. I hate it; his words punctuated by each smack.

"You have a right to your opinion; you don't have a right to embarrass me in public. I don't do it to you; you won't do it to me screaming like some petulant, spoiled brat, throwing wine on me, that's unacceptable." Smack, smack, smack, smack. My tears are salty, wet and hot – streaming down my face. I have been whipped, beaten, tortured. It doesn't compare to being spanked by somebody you love. And I do love him, I realize it again and again. My emotions are raw as I tell him I won't do it again.

"I'm sorry, I'm sorry." I plead hoping he will slow down, but he just continues. "Please, Jon, I'm sorry. I won't do it again." I know this won't stop until he chooses to stop it; in that moment, I can't stand him even though I love him. My rear end is on fire. It's embarrassing; my own father hasn't done this since I was a small child. I realize that he has stopped, and I'm just lying on his lap. His hand that delivered punishment earlier is just lightly rubbing my back.

I don't hate him, but I don't want to face him either. This is one of the most embarrassing parts of our relationship. In five short minutes, he takes me back to my childhood when all I had to worry about was getting spanked by Papa. Jon has no idea all that has transpired since that innocent time. But, I am not a child and what he would do when he realized that those fading scars he never speaks of are actually part of my KGB training.

And, what would Dragunov and Sobchak think if they knew I could be reduced to a balling child promising to be a good girl just to end a childish punishment. It was something they had missed preparing me for in all that brutal, cold training. They missed that and love – what happens to the agent when she falls for the man she's supposed to be extracting information from and manipulating?

I close my eyes against the reality of my life.

Jon stands me up, starring directly in my eyes. "Open your eyes, Lexy." I want to scurry off and hide, but he doesn't let me. His hands are on my shoulders, he shakes me slightly. "I don't disrespect you that way, and it's unacceptable for you to disrespect me. Is that clear?"

"Yes," I whisper.

"You are not to go out drinking tonight, either. Is that clear, Lexy?" *What is he, a mind reader?* That's all I want to do now, to get rid of the feelings of being loved when I was a child. I can't dwell on those days too much. I just want to get drunk and slosh away the vulnerability those feelings produce.

"Aren't you staying tonight?" We had made plans to spend a lovely evening together. Now that this has happened, I want him to hold me even more.

"No." Great, he's still angry.

"Oh," I can't keep the disappointment out of my voice.

"I expect to see you bright and early tomorrow morning. Understand?" *He's leaving me. Don't they all leave me? My family, my friends, my future.* I feel the desolation and despair folding in on me again. I try to hide it, but I know my eyes reflect my feelings. Discipline holds my tears in check, but just barely.

Maybe, I'll just go out and get drunk anyway. What the hell.

I realize that Jon is looking at me with that thoughtful look he gets sometimes. He doesn't let me go; instead he picks me up and carries me to my bed. Pulling the blankets back, he places me on one side of the bed. "Get undressed, Lexy." I do as I'm told, not saying a word. I shrug into my sweat pants and t-shirt, and he puts the blankets on me. Then he starts taking off his shirt and pants. He stuffs his socks into his shoes, and looks down at me again. I feel very small and too vulnerable to be a Russian spy.

"I thought you were leaving?" I whisper. *Did he hear my thoughts?* Is that why he's staying?

Jon climbs in the bed with me, and turns me on my side, spooning up behind me and wrapping me up in the blankets, his arm over my waist. He kisses my neck softly.

"I am still very angry with you, Lexy. Now go to sleep," It's all he says.

CHAPTER NINE

Hope is the thing with feathers

That perches in the soul,

And sings the tune--without the words,

And never stops at all.

We have the weekend off: no speeches to prepare for, no people or organizations to meet with, just a normal, happy weekend where we can be to ourselves. I am so happy to spend time with Jon, just Jon and no one else.

My morning is bliss, bright, loving and lustful. Jon making slow, delicious love to me for what feels like hours, in ways I'd never dared imagine and some that I did. There's something to be said for sleeping with an older, more experienced man.

Afterwards we bathe together in his large bathtub, his strong arms drawing a soapy foam over my fatigued muscles, my nerves racing with little electrical explosions of delight as his hand washes my sensual areas. He lifts my feet from the water, kissing my wet toes, pressing them against his angular cheek, little stubs of whisker scratching and tickling my soles which sends me into fits of giggling.

Even with Jon completely clear of the gangland shootout, he says we're still not out of danger from the mob, although I think the KGB is the bigger enemy. I can't say that, but I know they must still be shadowing us. Jon thinks we are being followed; perhaps by the original gang Jon was trying to bamboozle in the first place. I worry that if they suspect Jon was working with rivals, whom Dragunov convincingly framed by leaving one of their soldiers dead at the scene, they'll blame Jon even though they'd intended to ambush him in the first place.

"No. The guys I was negotiating with got wacked. That means the whole matter has to be reconsidered. More likely than not, they're regrouping and moving on to something else, probably taking care of that other crime family." Jon's words are not reassuring.

"Then why wouldn't they want to take you out, too?"

He looks at me, a half-smile seemingly amused by my use of murder lingo, "It's risky to take out a person like me. That hit may not even have been authorized. Anyway, it's not like we'll be entirely alone."

I think about it, worried. The KGB is shadowing me, probably shadowing Jon too, and Dragunov, with a whole second squad of goons maybe shadowing them. Now, we're going to have a third contingent of people shadowing the shadows. *This is getting a bit too complicated.*

However, before I can kick my worry beads into high, panicked gear, Jon explains. "I've got some special operatives I've already arranged to shadow me. They won't be intrusive, but they'll be around." Great, we now have so many people following us, we'll need a second or third car to put them all in. The image is funny – Russian spies, Mafia thugs and Jon's special forces all riding behind us in black sedans trying to look inconspicuous. With all of those people on our trail, it will be impossible to miss them. It's a funny notion, but my terrorized soul finds no humor in it.

"You've got people undercover, private security?" I instantly review the past weeks. *What could they have seen me do? Who could they have seen me talking to?* Knowing this could be very bad for me, I wait for Jon to explain further, so I'll know if I'm off the hook or hoisted upon my own petard.

"They're not mine, *per se.* I made a call, put 'em on kind of a standby basis. Just think of it as a little extra protection."

"Like an insurance policy."

He kisses my hand and a tiny charge thrills up my arm, hairs standing up on the back of my neck. "Exactly. But let's not worry about that right now. I want to show you Washington. Have you ever seen the monuments and museums here?"

I shake my head no. When did I have time to go sightseeing?

"Well, let's rectify that. Let's have breakfast and go see the sights. I'll be your guide."

"Okay," I reply. *Sightseeing.* It is the last thing I want to do, walking around town looking at old, dusty statues while some overly animated drone speaks a rehearsed speech about the wonders of democracy being born. I yawn to myself, and go get dressed. *There will probably be a line of shadows following us around. Won't they be bored.*

We visit the monuments; Lincoln's determined glare cutting through the ages and beyond; Jefferson, standing in frozen eloquence; Washington's ivory spire. The tour reminds me of the statues in Moscow, the stone saints of the Vatican's St. Peter's Basilica, which I'd seen pictures of as a child. America seems to be taking its place for me among those ancient empires, as surely as it has taken its place among the current giants on the world stage. *Well, better to think of it that way than to be bored silly, which I am.*

I watch Jon gazing at these monuments, which speak even

more clearly to him than to me. His smile melts away and he gazes solemnly, reverently, as if in the presence of the men these monuments represent. He seems sensitive to their presence from beyond the grave. As if he might glean some an insight from their lofty heights, peeking behind the curtain of life's mysteries. It's a nice sentiment, but I'm still bored.

After monument crawling, Jon takes me dancing, but not to the loud clubs I'd visited weeks before. He spins me across the dance floor of an elegant ballroom, where ladies and gentlemen in the finest evening wear twirl and flutter in a kind of aristocratic ballet. I feel somewhat inadequate in my dress; many women are wearing fancy ball gowns. Jon says it's fine, and that I'm beautiful. After seeing other women in shorter dresses, I relax into the magical evening where I'm being swept away like I'm in a fairy-tale.

Jon is masterful, handsome and dignified and in control as he leads me, through a series of dizzying dance steps like the Tango. the Flamenco and an old fashioned waltz.

My body is his to command, guiding me in steps that have traced the journeys of a million lovers before us, and will keep doing so for the millions of lovers that will follow. The music pulses through me, my legs strong as they match Jon's steps, feeling bouncy and committed, my hair loose around my head as I snap and spin and dip.

As we swirl across the floor, I'm drawn to the men standing at the edges of the dance floor. Most are smiling, talking to the women attending them and laughing at jokes I can't hear. In addition, I see two men, dressed in dark pants, white shirts and dark blazers. Each is smoking a cigarette watching – watching me and Jon, I realize. As we twirl away on the strands of waltz music, I know they are KGB as surely as I know that I love the man I'm dancing with.

They are watching and waiting for orders to kill. As we come around again, I see that they are gone. Will they kill Jon? I wonder and the thought sickens me. I am running out of time, and for all the wonder and beauty of my life here in the seat of American democracy, I feel the Russian world closing in on me.

I must make a decision, and I must make it soon.

###

BOOK 2 Coming In May 2016

If you would like to be notified when Robert Furst & Alan Parker have new releases, sign up on our mailing list.

www.fictionbuzzpress.com

"We're born alone, we live alone, we die alone. Only through our love and friendship can we create the illusion for the

moment that we're not alone." -- Orson Welles

If you enjoyed this novel, please leave a review for my book. we would greatly appreciate it.

ABOUT THE AUTHORS

Robert Furst owns his own construction company, and has been in the business for nigh on 20 years. A successful entrepreneur, husband and father, he has always had a dream to write fiction. His two daughters are nearly grown – Chloe is a freshman at Temple University and Brittany is in her third year of high school. Brittany aspires to be a writer one day, and at her urging, her father wrote his first novel, Intimate Enemies along with his best friend, Alan Parker.

Alan Parker is the exact opposite of his longtime friend, Robert Furst. He is an accountant working for one of the premiere law firms in Philadelphia. He writes for relaxation, and has loved the craft since he was in college. While his contribution was less than Roberts, he contributed great ideas and wrote many of the earlier scenes in the book, leaving the romance portion to Robert, and at points, his daughter Brittany.